AF559808

VIGILANTE KILLERS (Series)

Tara India Research Press introduces its new series and double collection of the Vigilante Killers...

A series of perfect murders...

Their MOs are undetectable, their methodology perfect. One wanted to lead a simple life, the other knew it was not for her. Each in her own way found her calling... to right the wrong, and their work goes on.

Two women – Two killers – Two books

Housewife

The housewife turns vigilante. As filth pours out from various pores of the city, she takes on the responsibility of cleaning it up. The housewife, the homemaker, has become the new lawmaker in the city. But soon she will have to face the ultimate test. One that will rock her very foundations. Can she balance her unique power and her 'homemaker' heart?

The Girl With the Poison Touch

A dead lab techie in Ahmedabad.
A mafia don shot in Shimla.
A reformed cricketer collapses on the field in Cuttack. The three of them have nothing in common. Never have their paths crossed. And yet, all of them were targets!!
Kavita knows Rana. What he looks like and that he is a tough customer. Rana doesn't know anything about Kavita. But he knows the answer lies in the histories of the men. Will he succeed in catching her, or will 'Killer Kavita' elude him?

HOUSEWIFE

HOUSEWIFE

Mahendra Jakhar

4 HOUR BOOKS

an imprint of tara press

4 Hour Books
An imprint of Tara Press

Flat 6, Khan Market, New Delhi - 110 003
Ph.: 24694610; Fax : 24618637
www.indiaresearchpress.com
contact@indiaresearchpress.com

2022

ISBN 13 : 978-81-8386-174-8

Printed and Bound in India

1

There was a spring in her step as she walked over the cobbled streets of Colaba, Mumbai. The title track from *Pretty Woman* played in her head as she smiled to herself. She sported a flowery dress and a bright red lipstick that she saved for special occasions. It was date night after months.

She walked inside Leopold Café, one of the busiest joints in the area, and sat at a table in the centre. The place was overflowing with backpackers from across the world, a few middle-aged businessmen who had come to feast their eyes on *firangi* girls, and young college couples trying their hand at dating for the first time.

Antara checked herself on her mobile. In

spite of being one of the most popular cafés, Leopold didn't have an air-conditioner and fans whirred above the customers instead. Antara didn't want to sweat and get her eye-liner flowing all over her face, so she kept dabbing the sweat beads that appeared on her forehead. She was waiting for Vivek to come.

She could feel the eyes of men on her. It was like a shot of confidence. It was after months that she felt beautiful. Nothing wrong with that, a girl needs to be appreciated, secretly eyed and showered with compliments, of course, within limits. That's what differentiated gentlemen from rowdies and the game of flirting from lechery. The whole process of winning over a girl has to be gentle and slow and needs to be played, taking it a notch higher with every step. At times naughty and at times romantic. At times being crazy and at others being a quiet listener or simply a boyfriend, a lover, a Romeo, a Majnu, a father and grandfather all rolled into one and scoring points at every step to win the woman.

Antara wanted to play the game all over again with her husband tonight. She had spent a lot of time on her hair and make-up. She had taken the first step in the game. She wanted to make it fun and ignite the dying spark in their dull, married life. She had carefully thought and planned all the things to say to Vivek, all the things that they would do together, exactly what they would eat before heightening the game in the night. It would be beautiful after a long time. In fact, whenever she thought of her happy life, it was like, once upon a time... Tonight was the chance of her lifetime to make it shine again.

She smiled at the waiter gently, parting her lush red lips to ask him for a cold coffee. It was always awkward to sit at a table waiting for someone. At least an order stopped the waiters from coming to ask if you wanted something, again and again.

The waiter had just got her cold coffee when, with it, came in three masked men. They were carrying automatic guns and, without wasting a second, started shooting at the people all around the cafe.

The bullets tore through bodies and shattered furniture and fixtures. The whole place was filled with cries and drowned in blood. They targeted all the white people before turning their guns on the others.

Antara could see her life coming to an end. There was no place to run or hide. She could see the bullets flying past her and tearing through the bodies of men and women as she sat on the floor under the table.

Finally, she saw the guns pointed at her. All her dreams and her life seemed to evaporate in that moment. One final attempt. She threw her handbag at them and got up to run. The guns responded with a volley of fire and ripped her apart.

2

Antara woke up with a start, tears rolling down her face. She checked herself to see if she was hurt and looked around to find that she was fine and lying in bed. It was another one of those nightmares.

She looked at the wall clock. It was 11.40 p.m. She could hear the faint hum of the television coming from the living room.

She walked out hurriedly and saw Vivek glued to the television, watching the news. A bearded reporter stood in front of Leopold Cafe, reporting the terror attack in the city, as a police team carried away bodies. Three terrorists had attacked Leopold Cafe, killing over twenty people and injuring more than thirty.

She was stunned. It was exactly as she had seen in her dream.

"I saw this in my dream tonight," she blurted.

"Antara, please. I don't want to hear about your weird dreams. You had better stop watching those horror and detective shows that you are so fond of. I have to hurry and follow up on this news," said Vivek, buttoning his shirt.

"I told you this is happening again and again. Whatever I see in my dream somehow comes true," Antara persisted.

Vivek turned to look at her and smiled. He kept his hands on her shoulders and said, "Okay, say for a moment that I believe you. Tell me, where are these terrorists hiding? The entire police force is looking for them. Maybe you can help them nab those terrorists."

Antara looked at him and said, "I woke up as they started to shoot at me."

"And yet you are right here in front of me, without a scratch on your body," said Vivek. "I have been telling you to not pay too much attention to these dreams. You need to do something constructive, something productive in your life, otherwise your life is a waste. I mean examine your daily routine, everything you do—from cooking food, washing clothes, dusting, supervising the maids, shopping, vegetable chopping, again cooking, and yes, watching lots of television and web series, films and repeat. This is your life. I'm a journalist and I have a responsibility to serve the society, and I do my best. You have no interests, no friends, no hobbies, and with all this talk of dreams, you are creating a fantasy world for yourself. Get out of this rut and get into some productive work. I have to leave now."

Vivek picked up his bag to leave and said, "Don't venture out into shopping malls and markets. You don't know where these terrorists might be hiding."

Antara nodded quietly behind Vivek.

She stood there, lost in thought. *"What productive work can I do? I'm just a housewife who seems to be losing her mind."*

3

Antara Sachdeva, 35 years old, had been undergoing IVF treatment for the last six months. Her in-laws blamed her for not being able to conceive. She had given up her flourishing public relations career to take on the full-time role of a housewife. However, she had given up hope of being a mother. She could sense her biological clock ticking and finally opted to have an IVF baby. The treatment was a painful process of many injections and things being put inside her.

She thought that it was due to the heavy doses of medication that she was getting these weird dreams, or were they hallucinations? It was only recently that she realised that these were not dreams, that she saw actual events happening in real time. She often tried her best to pull her mind away from them and call up her mother in Patel Nagar, Delhi, instead, for mega talkathons.

It was almost eleven years since her wedding and six years since they shifted to the eighteenth-floor apartment of Gokuldham Society in Goregaon East, Mumbai. Vivek worked as an assistant editor with a television news channel, News 24x7, and was responsible for selecting and gathering daily stories. He had a team of twelve reporters working under him and he made sure they brought him sensational stories.

Vivek and Antara had met at a party hosted by a large corporate house whose public relations was being handled by Antara. It was a hot love affair and within two years they were married. Over time, as Vivek realised that Antara could not conceive, he became distant, and with time, more and more aloof. He drowned himself in work and made sure that the channel he worked for was riding high on the TRP charts.

Every day Antara finished her housework by 12.30 p.m. and spent the next two hours on her cosmetic rituals. Late afternoons were meant for binge-watching television shows and movies. In the evenings she tried going out for long walks but could not keep up with them due to her IVF treatment that exhausted her both mentally and physically.

She looked young, with an oval face and bright black eyes and shoulder-length black hair. She preferred to dress in Punjabi suits as they were snug and had comfortably sunk into the role of a housewife.

By the time she finished watching *Jab We Met* for the twentieth time, it was seven-thirty in the evening. Often she would fantasize about Vivek being more romantic, bringing her flowers, chocolates and gifts and making love to her in the living room. However, she had long ago given up on all these notions. She was a normal, boring, unromantic housewife.

Except that she failed in the most important aspect of that role, that of a mother. Something many other women reminded her of with their taunts and questions about when she was giving everyone the "good news". And so she had contained herself in her own world of television, books, dreams, treatments, and her parents and in-laws.

Antara's cell phone rang and she saw it was her mother calling. Rajshri Batra, 65 years, ran a boutique in Karol Bagh. She had come a long way from running a small cloth shop in Chawri Bazaar. She made sure that her boutique catered to all age groups and would keep the latest Bollywood designs.

"I haven't been able to breathe since I heard about this terror attack in Mumbai and you don't even have the decency to call me? I have been chanting Mata Rani's name and only in the evening when I heard that the police had killed those terrorists did I have a sip of chai. How do you live in that dirty city filled with garbage and broken roads? Why don't you tell Vivek to take a transfer to Delhi and we can all be together?" her mother ranted as Antara answered the phone.

"We are fine, don't worry. Vivek is doing really good here," said Antara.

Her mother rattled off again, "What about you? What are you doing? From the time you left your job, you have become careless. I have started doing yoga and you too should start doing it. You should go on walks morning and evening, or better yet, join a gym. I have bought some dry fruits for you and have designed a new backless blouse that I will courier to you."

"Why do you keep sending me these

blouses? You know I don't wear all this," said Antara.

"*Haan*, you have become even more old-fashioned than me. At your age you need to look hot and sexy. You should get those tights and show a little of your butt. Men love that."

"Mummy, enough of all this gyan. I have lot of work here. I'll talk to you later," said Antara and cut the call. She looked out and saw that it was evening already and the sky had turned grey. She sat down on the sofa and flipped through a book. She switched on the TV and browsed through news channels.

She was bored and sad.

Antara opened the sliding doors of the large windows and saw the red tail lights of vehicles spread out on the road like embers. She loved these late evenings, when the dark blue sky merged with the multi-hued city lights. She could see the Oberoi Mall glittering in all its splendour and the many under-construction buildings rising up like giants in the sky.

She stepped over the window-sill and walked out. She saw children playing in the society, cycling, running, and the mothers howling to keep them in check. Antara looked around and realised that she was walking on thin air outside her window, eighteen floors above the ground.

For a moment she thought that she would fall. She moved around, tiptoeing, did a quick dance step, and laughed. She walked ahead and her foot touched a high-tension wire running parallel to the road. It freaked her out and she cried, but realised that nothing had happened.

She touched the wire again. Nothing. Slowly, she placed one foot on the wire and then the other. Like a tight-rope walker, she started to walk on the wire from Film City Road right up to the Oberoi Mall flyover. In between, she jumped and danced and did a jig like gymnasts on a balancing beam. She was thrilled and excited.

She jumped down and walked over the roofs of the cars speeding towards the traffic light. As she jumped down, a truck rammed into her and sped away. She sat on the road with eyes popping out and the vehicles passing all over her. She seemed to be made of air, or light. Nothing affected her. She saw this and got up, looking as cars dashed into and sped out of her. She was like the ghost she had seen in the movies.

"What if this is a dream?" she woke up with a jolt as she thought of her house. *"Now, what?"*

In the next instant, she was standing in her living room. She looked around for herself and without realizing it, walked through the wall into the bedroom. She saw herself sleeping on the sofa, a book lying half open on the side. A cookery show was playing on the television.

She was shell-shocked. *If that is Antara, who am I?*

4

The very first thought that hit her was whether she was dead and it was only her body that was lying on the sofa. She had seen this kind of scene in many movies.

She started to cry. "I'm dead. I don't want to die, God. Please, I want to live more."

She bent closer to look at Antara, who was sleeping on the sofa. She could hear the faint snoring. Vivek had often told her to stop snoring but she would always say, "I don't snore."

So, she was alive. She edged closer to Antara's body and hesitatingly extended her finger to touch it.

The moment she touched the body, she vanished, and Antara woke up.

"What the hell is happening to me?" She looked around to see if someone else was there in the room. She got scared of her own self. She realised that the other her had merged into her body and they had become one. *Is it like those horror movies where a spirit had taken possession of her?* She started to chant the gayatri mantra.

Antara was filled with fear and slowly turned to look at herself in the mirror. She was exactly the same. There were no changes in her body, her face or her eyes. Nothing seemed contorted like they showed in movies when one is possessed by a spirit.

She sat down and tried talking to herself. "Who the hell is inside me? You don't know me but I'm a big devotee of Lord Shiva. I am going to call on him and he'll throw you out of me and into hell."

Nothing happened. No sounds. No twisting of the body or the rolling of eyes. Nothing protruded from inside her body. No change in voice. No flying objects in the room. No thunder or lightning.

Damn!

She sat there, quietly waiting for some sign of a spirit possessing her. She felt as normal as ever. She hurriedly rose and lit the diya in the pooja place, all the while chanting *Om Namah Shivay.*

She called up Vivek on his cell phone. "Vivek, I'm scared. You know I was sleeping and I saw this..."

Vivek cut her off saying, "Antara, stop watching those silly television shows. I have had enough of your dreams. I'm trying to work here and please don't bug me with these idiotic stories." With that he cut the call.

Antara stood there in silence. She felt numb. She had no idea what was happening to her. Was she hallucinating? Was she going crazy?

She walked into the living room, sat on the sofa, and closed her eyes. For the very first time in her life, she was examining herself. She tried to empty her mind and focus only on what was inside her.

Within a minute she slumped onto the sofa. She saw herself sprawled on it and realised that she was looking at her own body lying there.

"What am I?"

She went closer and touched the body on the couch. Instantly, she was fused with it again. And, Antara, the human, was up. "What the hell?"

She had touched the body and she was back to her normal self. So, this time she stood on the floor and closed her eyes to focus. In less than a minute, her body slumped to the floor like a rag and she stood watching it.

She walked closer to the body and touched it and in an instant she was back.

5

"Is it my soul, my atman, that moves out of my body?" thought Antara.

The big shocker was that she could do it at will. She could move in and out of her body in an instant. She tried to wrap her head around the whole thing and suddenly thought, *"What if this is a dream?"*

She pinched herself and cried out. It felt real. She looked out of the window to see the mothers calling out to their kids to get back home. She turned to look at the wall clock. It was 8.45, past her dinner time. Vivek usually came back home around 11, after wrapping up the 9 p.m. prime time show, *News Line*.

What she had discovered about herself

was so overpowering that she didn't feel like eating anything.

"Is this what they call occult powers?" thought Antara. She was just a normal housewife. And yet, she could control her spirit moving in and out of her body. In her spirit form, she could also travel anywhere she liked.

So, all those weird dreams were actually real, and it turned out that her spirit form travelled out and witnessed these horrific events.

A big smile spread on her face. She closed her eyes, focussing on her inner self. In an instant, the body fell and the spirit stood over it in all its glory. She walked to the large sliding windows and stepped out. There she stood, hanging in the air, watching the lights of the buildings for some time. She looked up at the building and started to walk on the walls. To her amazement, she stood straight and kept walking right up towards the roof. It was like being in a movie. She started to run and went right up to stand high on the roof of the forty-floor building.

She could almost see and hear the heavy wind at this height but didn't feel it. She stood there in her salwar-suit, like Spiderman or Batman, looking at her city. For the last few months, she had been telling Vivek to take her for a drive on the Bandra–Worli sea link. She thought of being there. The next second she was there, standing on top of a pillar of the sea link. She gasped at the traffic moving on the bridge and the sea waves rolling underneath.

For the first few moments she was scared of falling. Then she smiled. "I am a spirit. I cannot die. No one can see me."

Antara started to jump from one pillar to the other, dancing on the many lights. This was so much more beautiful than a drive on the bridge.

It'd been a while since Vivek had taken any interest in her. She had given up her career to be a housewife and a mother. She had continued to take all the pains of the IVF treatment but failed to conceive, and instead of being more loving and caring, Vivek had slowly withdrawn and distanced himself from her. They had become like couples who hardly spoke and communicated only in monosyllables.

Even the vacations had stopped. "It's the same mountains and beaches everywhere.

It would be better if you do something constructive with your life than take vacations," Vivek would tell her.

She sat on the highest pillar of the sea link thinking about their drowning relationship. She had tried her best to bring life and jest into it, but nothing seemed to work.

Most of their talk was about a leaky tap, a broken glass, bills, or the new furniture she had wanted to buy for the last three years. Everything inadvertently turned into an argument. After a while, she had resigned herself to fate and her role of this lifetime—being a housewife.

She felt drained of all the enthusiasm and energy she had felt at the discovery of her extraordinary power. After all, what could she do with this? Nothing more than move in and out of her body, roam around the city, dance and laugh. By the end of it, she had to get back into her body to fulfil the role of a good wife. Obviously, she couldn't live like a spirit. She was nothing more than a ghost in this form.

She had often wanted to visit Vivek at his office, to see him working, but he had never taken her there. She closed her eyes to picture his office and in an instant was inside Vivek's office.

She saw rows of monitors with the 9 p.m. show rolling on them. There were journalists, editors and technicians working on their desks. She looked around and walked through doors and equipment.

She saw a coffee cup fall and rushed to grab it but couldn't. She was shocked. She tried to pick up a pen from the desk but couldn't. Her hand would pass through them. She realised that she couldn't touch anything or pick up anything. She could watch, observe, and see things as they happened but could not do anything to change the outcome.

A little ahead was the studio with glass walls. She could see the anchor engaged in a heated debate with the guests. Vivek was standing near the camera as he gave a countdown for the next news item and directed the anchor to end the debate. Antara stood there, mesmerized, as the whole team worked to roll out the show and, after exactly eight minutes, went into a three-minute commercial break.

Vivek was filled with enthusiasm and energy as he gave a high five to the anchor and to his team for doing a great job. She could see him hugging a young female reporter and laughing with his team. This was the Vivek she had fallen in love with. At home, he never laughed or even smiled. This was his workplace and his team was his family, where he felt most alive and happy.

Antara could do nothing but blame herself for their failed relationship. She walked out as Vivek started to give the countdown for the next news item.

6

With a heavy heart, Antara sat on top of one of the tallest buildings in south Bombay. It was a sixty-five-storey building that housed corporate big-wigs, financial wizards, IT czars and a few Bollywood stars. The very power that gave her so much freedom suddenly made her feel lonely. Yes, she could move at the speed of thought, walk into any place, move through walls and glide through traffic. So what? Did that mean anything?

She felt no more than a street magician. In fact, she felt inferior to him. He could at least show his tricks to the crowd and please them.

She could feel the loneliness of superheroes. However, they still went out and fought the baddies and helped people.

Dressed in her salwar-suit, with her *chunri* flying in the wind, and her cheap rubber slippers, she started to walk on the outer wall of the building, going down. The building had huge five-bedroom apartments with each room opening onto a deck overlooking the sea. It was one of the most expensive properties in Mumbai.

She stopped near a massive glass window, watching a teenage party going on inside. The teeny-boppers were dancing to the tunes of Justin Bieber and Beyonce. These were the ones who had started experimenting with smoke, weed, alcohol and sex.

Antara kept walking and saw an elderly couple sitting at a distance on the sofa, watching television. She looked at them for a while, thinking, *"So, this is what we finally become. Distant. Silent. Dead."* She moved on, saying, "I don't want to be like them."

She descended further to see a young maid feeding two kids lying in bed while the mother stood in front of the mirror trying on her designer jewellery. Antara was enraged to see this. "If I had kids, I would have left everything to take care of them."

She walked down the wall of the building as the wind rushed past her. She could see tiny lights on the road twinkling at the base of the building. She was somewhere close to the fiftieth floor, taking her time to come down, soaking in the view.

She came close to a large deck and saw a middle-aged man shouting at a young woman. It was a luxurious house, perhaps on the fiftieth floor. The woman wore heavy diamond rings and diamond studs and was dressed in the most expensive designer dress. Her footwear seemed to shout out—don't touch me.

The man grabbed the woman's throat, shouting, "You were nothing till I married you and gave you this lavish lifestyle. You would have still been sleeping with various men to get some work if it wasn't for me. I gave you everything and now you talk back to me?"

Antara could see that the man was drunk and filled with rage. He kept shouting at the woman, calling her names. "You are nothing but my bitch. So you very well listen to me and do what I tell you to."

"I am not going to..." spoke the woman.

At the same moment, the man slapped her tight across the face. "Who the hell are you to decide what to do and what not to?" he shouted.

He slapped her again and grabbed her hair, saying, "Even if I throw you down from here, nothing is going to happen to me. I'll tell the police that you were a drug addict and died by suicide. Should I throw you down?"

The man started to push the woman towards the edge. She started to scream, "I'm sorry. I'm sorry." The man laughed out and said, "That's like my bitch." He pushed her down on the floor and kicked her in the ribs.

Antara saw this and rushed to intervene. She tried to stop the man but couldn't. She shouted but no one heard her. She stood in between the couple, but the man kicked again and it went right through her and hit the woman on her face.

The man bent close to his wife and said, "You know the deal with Raheja is worth thirty crores. You had better sleep with him and make him sign this deal."

"Please, I'm your wife," she cried.

He grabbed her throat again. "You are nothing more than my bitch and I'll toss you to each and every dog. Do exactly as I tell you or I'll make sure you land up homeless and penniless on the street."

With this he pulled her up. "You better strip and show me."

She looked at him, shocked, and he slapped her hard.

Antara tried to hold his hand, but the hand flew through her and hit the woman again and again. Antara turned to look at her. The woman was cowering in fear, tears streaking down her cheeks, filled with bruises. Antara extended her hand to wipe the woman's tears and suddenly she was inside her body.

Antara looked through the eyes of the woman and moved through her body. She realised she had entered the woman's body. As the man again raised his hand, Antara instinctively grabbed his hand mid-way. This brought a wide smile to her face and the grin showed on the woman's face.

The man was infuriated. "You dare smile at me? I will teach you to mock me. Let me see your teeth. I'm going to smash this smile off your face."

He swung his fist at the woman's face. Instead of whimpering in fear, Antara blocked the blow and twisted his arm. The man winced in pain. Antara kept twisting it and the man kept moving back till he hit the edge of the deck. He tried to free himself.

"I'm going to throw you down," he screamed.

At this, Antara pushed him. He was in the air. His body hurtled down fifty floors. She didn't even hear the thud of his body hitting the ground.

Shocked, Antara moved out of the woman's body and stood there. *"What have I done? I killed a man."* She turned to look at the woman who was lying unconscious on the deck.

7

Vivek was lying in bed, fast asleep. Antara was on the other side of the bed, almost lifeless, wide awake. She noticed Vivek on her side and suddenly everything came rushing back to her. She had pushed a man from the balcony of the fiftieth floor. He couldn't have survived. She had turned into a killer.

She got out of bed and walked to the bathroom. She made sure to lock the door from inside and examined herself for any signs that might get the police chasing her. She washed her hands with a large amount of hand wash. She looked at her face and neck for any signs of a scuffle.

Nothing.

She turned on the shower tap and stood under it in her salwar-suit, letting the cold water soak her body, getting rid of all the smell, signs or evidence. She stood there for almost ten minutes and realised the society president would question each and every person going out of the building, "Who wasted so much water? More than half the tank is empty." She quickly turned off the shower and sat down on the floor.

Each and every action replayed in her mind. She could see the woman pleading, the man abusing her. Then, somehow, she had entered the woman's body and, in trying to protect her, twisted his arm and pushed him down. She shivered. She had turned into a ghost-like figure like in the movies, who possesses other people and makes them do things against their will. However, this was not a movie. She was real.

She was a spirit with a body which she could discard like a pile of clothes and move out of at will. Now she had discovered that could enter other bodies and make them do things. A faint smile appeared on her face. "No one saw me. It was my spirit and the other woman who pushed her husband down."

She almost laughed out at the thought. *"So I can enter other bodies. That's the way I can touch, feel and act. Maybe this is the way I can do something. Finally, God has been kind to me and has shown me a way to use my power. But what can I do? Maybe I can rob a bank? Or, what if I enter the body of our ministers and make them say crazy things on news channels? Vivek will be thrilled."*

Antara jumped up like a kid. She could be anybody and make them do anything. This was her extraordinary power. Finally she could be like those superheroes and get a name for herself.

She started thinking of names—Super Antara, Super Aunty, Wonder Girl, Spirit Girl, Super Soul, or something to do with woman power.

Suddenly, she realised that she had completely forgotten about the other woman who had fallen unconscious on the balcony floor. *"I hope she is fine."*

8

"Amrit Shah, aged 53, fell headlong to the ground of the Alta Mount building from his fiftieth-floor balcony. He was drunk. There were few Ecstasy tablets in his trouser pockets. It appears that he had a cocktail of drugs and alcohol that made him lose control. Amrit Shah came home around 9 p.m. and got into an argument with his twenty-seven-year-old wife, Leena, which turned into a quarrel. According to Leena, her husband started to abuse and beat her. He pushed her onto the balcony and kicked her many times, after which she lost consciousness. It seems that Amrit, under the influence of drugs and alcohol, lost his balance thinking that he had killed Leena and jumped from the balcony to his death. It appears to be a clear case of suicide," the police report said.

A similar small report appeared in the newspaper. Vivek read the news while sipping his morning tea and started to call his reporters to do a follow-up story. He knew Amrit Shah was a leading businessman who financed many Bollywood films and had huge stakes in many businesses and successful start-ups. As per *Forbes India*, he was worth over ten thousand crore. He had married a young starlet and had affiliations with political parties, even hawala channels. It was said that he had made most of his money during the demonetisation days. He charged 15 per cent for the exchange of old five-hundred and thousand-rupee notes. From that alone he had made more than five hundred crore rupees in less than two weeks.

A few dailies reported that he had been under financial stress after a few of his investments had tanked and had borrowed loads of money to keep his business afloat. However, no one knew the real truth. In such cases, rumours fly and stories are created to keep the suicide of a top business tycoon alive. They get to call interesting guests and celebrities and question and debate on many false theories, all to grab eyeballs. That's what the media had become; it wanted to grab you by your balls with whatever stories it dished out, even if they were made up.

That morning, Vivek decided to dig deeper into this. He suspected that it wasn't suicide. He had earlier interviewed Amrit Shah and found him to be a man who loved all the extravagance and power that came with his money. He couldn't have jumped to his death. He was one man who literally loved to live his life. He was certainly not depressed.

Antara, too, hurriedly went through the small news item with the headline: 'Cash King falls to death'. She was relieved to see that the police had declared it a suicide. Amrit's wife was taken care of and was doing well. As she went through Amrit's story, Antara felt that she had done nothing wrong. He was not only a wife-beater but a man who had cheated many people to fill his coffers. He was a fifty-three-year-old fat, ugly, abusive and manipulative man who married a young actress for her looks and body. Leena was his trophy wife to be showcased in corporate circles but beaten and raped and spitted at behind closed doors.

"Good riddance, Amrit Shah," thought Antara. *"Humanity won't miss you."* Whatever little guilt she had felt vanished and she felt empowered.

"Antara, pack my breakfast. I'll eat it in the car. I am on this very important story," Vivek interrupted her thought.

He moved out of the room and Antara handed him his office bag and a few sandwiches wrapped in foil. "Thanks. I hope you are not getting any of those weird dreams. Take care," he said as he stepped out, without even looking back. Antara stood inside the house, looking at the door shut on her face.

This was their daily routine. They exchanged these words and found some life in them. The relationship was dead. Antara had read article after article on how to rekindle the romance. The articles assured her that it was like a mid-life crisis and would soon be over.

She had tried many of the things she read—dress sexily, plan vacations, watch romantic movies together, say sweet nothings, indulge in pillow and sex talk, gift flowers, and chocolates, but nothing had worked. Every day she would chalk out ten points to bring back love and laughter in their lives, but with dismal returns. They had even gone for their second and third honeymoons. The relationship was dead. Their mid-life crisis had become a lifelong thing.

Apart from her not being able to conceive, Antara felt that Vivek thought of her as a good-for-nothing, typical housewife. He didn't even show any interest in spending time with her, let alone taking her out for movies and shopping. Many a times he had told her to do something worthwhile in her life.

"Go get a life. Do something productive. I am a journalist at heart. News is my passion. It gives me a kick. What do you like? What is the purpose of your life? In what way are you contributing to society? Do something constructive," Vivek had told her often.

She walked to the newspaper lying on the table and picked it up. She saw the news item about Amrit Shah's suicide. "This is my contribution to the society," Antara said to herself. "I clean the filth of this society."

With that, she threw the newspaper away and stood frozen on the spot. "Maybe this is my purpose. Maybe this is the reason I have been given this power. Maybe I can clean up more filth."

9

Leena preferred to call herself by her first name. She had never used Amrit Shah's surname. It had got noticed somewhere and the media called her a strong-willed woman who stood for herself with a thinking head on her shoulders. However, Leena didn't give the media any access to her private life.

Vivek tried desperately to get a personal interview but she did not respond to his many requests.

It was a week since Amrit's suicide. The media had been playing a guessing game, fabricating all sorts of stories about Leena and her relationship with the man. One of the news channels went to the length of describing Leena as a lesbian and others called Amrit a drug addict who was into young boys. It was strange that in a country where cinema was so strictly censored, there was no censorship for these news channels. They made their own rules and turned debates into gladiatorial contests. They passed verdicts and assassinated people's characters.

Leena had survived because she had refused to give into their games. She had kept herself protected and locked away from the prying eyes of these vultures. So it was a field day for the media when Leena announced that she would be taking over as the new CEO of Lotus Enterprises, her husband's business. She had called a press conference at the head office and the entire hall was packed.

Vivek was there with his team in the hope that he might get to do the very first interview with her. In fact, everyone was there for the same reason.

Leena walked in surrounded by her black-clad security guards who seemed to be hired from an international security agency. She was dressed in a sharp business suit. She didn't smile or wave at the press. She looked calm, with a steely face. She sat in front of the army of reporters and the many mikes thrust near her face. They didn't want to miss a word.

Along with her sat the senior-most member of the board of directors. Everyone seemed to have given a nod to her taking over as the CEO. Leena started to speak in a clear, concise manner without any sign of emotion or nervousness. She talked in brief about the company, her role, her vision as the CEO and she announced that she had divided the whole company into three parts—Finance, Sports and Entertainment.

The reporters were on their feet, their mouths spewing questions at her. She didn't seem to listen to any of them. She calmly waited for them to quieten down and elaborated on the three areas. She announced that the company had taken a decision to have their own IPL Cricket team and would be bringing in the best of international cricketers to be part of it. The entertainment side would produce Bollywood and international movies with the most reputed names while the finance division would continue to function as before.

Once done, she swiftly moved out from

a door right behind the podium, leaving the media looking like a pack of wolves who had just been given bits of meat and were now hungry for more.

10

Obsessed with Amrit Shah's suicide case, Vivek had started chasing Leena everywhere. It had made him more irritable and short-tempered, especially with his chief editor pressuring him that the channel had to be the first to get 'that woman' on air.

Antara bore the brunt and got shouted at for the smallest things. She felt lonelier and more isolated than ever. She was trying her last bit to give her all to this relationship and she finally gave up.

In an attempt to escape, she started experimenting more with her powers. She travelled all across the city and saw all the places she had never seen. She always wanted to sit for hours by the sea and now she could do it at any time. She walked on top of Gateway of India, moved inside the most luxurious suites of Taj Palace Hotel and sat alongside top Bollywood stars inside their houses. She sat inside the Mantralaya, Maharashtra's legislative assembly building, hearing the many ministers making speeches or raising allegations.

It was like the whole city had opened its belly for her to look into. She could see but couldn't do anything. She would need a body to make it act as per her will. She went inside police stations and saw policemen taking bribes, torturing small-time criminals and blackmailing women to give in to their demands. She couldn't just start killing each and every corrupt man.

She walked into a five-star luxury hospital and saw a doctor telling the nurse that the patient on bed number eleven was already dead, but that they should keep him for another two days and keep the family at bay by saying that the patient was on ventilator and the doctors were doing everything to help him. The nurse had nodded quietly.

The whole city seemed corrupt. Be it the police, politicians, doctors, engineers, bankers, builders, auto-drivers, or even government officials, everyone was looking to make a quick buck. They had no respect or compassion for others. It was a dog-eat-dog city.

She was at a loss. She wanted to make a difference in people's lives and had already killed a vile man. Should she randomly choose and kill evil people, or should she start with the top government officials who made the policies and laws? The politicians, the bureaucrats, corporate giants, or terrorists—the list would be endless.

In her spirit form, she wandered from place to place, wondering, questioning. She walked through slums and saw drunken men abusing their wives, slum kids fighting over discarded plastic bottles, teenage boys eyeing young girls and women engaged in hard labour.

Antara was tired of seeing the sick city. She chose to go back home, cook, and wait for Vivek. She prepared a lavish dinner and waited for her husband as she wanted to enjoy the meal with him.

By the time he came home, it was 11.45 p.m. "I'm too tired and I have eaten in office," he said. He changed and was asleep in the next ten minutes.

Antara sat there looking at all the dishes laid out on the dining table. It'd been days since they had even touched each other. She forced herself to eat a few spoonfuls.

The ritual was the same in the morning. She handed him a packed breakfast. "Okay, bye, take care." The three words she got to hear every morning. The door shut on her face. Silence. Loneliness. Boredom.

Good-for-nothing housewife.

Antara went to her bedroom and lay on the bed. She concentrated within and in an instant her spirit was out. She wanted to see the fate of other such women, housewives. *"Is everyone so bored and lonely?"*

The next moment she was sitting inside the house of a middle-aged mother running around to pack lunchboxes for her school-going kids. Her husband called out to her to get him his black shoes. The husband was complaining that he knew she wasted a lot of time chatting with other women and gossiping about their men.

The woman started to polish his shoes while he warned her to stay at home and take care of the kids. The woman spent the next fifteen minutes scurrying around to get her chores done. Finally, the door shut. Everyone was gone. She was all alone. She breathed a sigh of relief. She sat down on the sofa and for the first time took a sip of her cold tea. She didn't even bother to heat it up. She had a long list of chores to be finished through the day and didn't even want to look at it. She put the cup down and closed her eyes.

Antara could feel her pain, her hollowness, and her sacrifice that amounted to nothing, a life given up to keep their family happy and together.

This was a housewife—a cook, a maid, a cleaner, a mother, a wife, a free sex worker and a punching bag all rolled into one. Still, she was a wasted life. She didn't go out to earn. She was not productive. She was not constructive. Only the men were.

The spirit form wanted to touch the woman, give her some comfort, but Antara managed to keep herself away. She wanted to disappear from there.

She was inside a small flat of another couple the next moment. The husband was shouting at his wife and slapping her continuously. A little boy hid in a corner with tears rolling down his cheeks.

"I saw you talking to that boy from Delhi. What were you doing with him? Are you getting attracted to these young boys now? I have doubts if this boy here is even my child?" shouted the man and pushed her down.

The woman straightened herself up, "Please don't say such things. I swear by our child, I have nothing to do with other men. I met that Delhi boy in the lift and he started talking to me about films. He has come to Mumbai to become an actor."

The husband kicked her in the stomach, shouting, "You were always crazy about movies and filmy people. How do I know you are not sleeping with him?"

The woman fell to the floor, as her husband continued to rain kicks on her. The little boy, hiding in the corner, couldn't bear it anymore. He jumped on his father, crying, "Don't hit my mother."

The man turned to the boy and slapped him hard. "How dare you touch me?" he shouted, pushing the child away and into the wall.

The mother leapt onto the man to save the child and tried to stop him from targeting the boy even further, but her futile attempts lasted only a few seconds before the husband brought her down by pulling her hair with one hand, slapping her left and right with the other.

Antara stood in a corner, watching. She hoped there were many who were happy and blissful. She was yet to see them. She wanted to pick up the little boy and hug him but something in her was stirring. She saw the man pick up his dirty office bag and heavy lunch box and leave the mother and child, crying inside the house.

The mother sobbed, hugging the boy, and cried, "I'm sorry. I'm sorry."

The only thing a helpless woman, mother and a housewife could do to comfort her kid in the face of such abuse.

The man took an auto-rickshaw to the nearest station to board a local train to Churchgate.

He stepped out of the auto-rickshaw outside the station. His eyes were glued to his cheap smart phone. Antara walked close to him as he watched a porn clip. It disgusted her so much that she wanted to spit at him.

The roads around the station were dug

up and everyone had to walk around the pits to go inside the station. An electricity pole had leaned in as the area around it was dug up and electric wires were hanging low.

Antara looked at the man and she could only remember him beating his wife and child. She gently tapped him on the shoulder and in an instant the spirit was inside his body. The eyes turned bright. He stepped ahead, shouting, "I am sorry. I'm sorry. I beat my wife and my child. Please forgive me."

With that he grabbed the electric wire hanging from the tilted pole. His entire body contorted as high voltage current ran through it. The huge crowd of people stopped to watch as sparks flew out of his body. The hand that grabbed the wire had burnt beyond recognition. His eyes had come out of their sockets and he fell to the ground with a thud. He tried to say something, but no words came out.

Antara moved out of his body. She stood there for a moment and then disappeared. She was clear in her heart – the man deserved this punishment. Good that she didn't kill him. There would be enough time to kill.

11

It was 11.30 p.m. when Vivek stepped into the rattling lift of his building. The old lift groaned and complained as it trudged up to their eighteenth-floor flat. Most of the elderly men and women of the society were in awe of him. Whenever they met him, they would call out to him and give him long feedback on his show. They wanted him to focus on the poor quality of roads, the constant digging in Mumbai, and the dust that filled the air. Vivek always promised to do the stories, but roads, air and pollution had been done to death; it wasn't sexy anymore. There was no spice in it, no zing. He was looking for a bigger scandal to cement his position in the news world.

Vivek stepped out of the lift and walked

up to his flat. Like always, he rang the bell and stood outside, waiting for Antara to open the door. There was no response. He again rang the bell and waited. Still, the door didn't open. Usually, he could hear Antara moving through the bedroom towards the living room, dragging her feet over the tiled floor.

There was no sound.

He was tired after a long day and getting irritated. He took out his set of keys and opened the door to step inside. The whole house was dark. There was no sign of Antara. He stood inside, looking through the darkness and called out to Antara.

No response.

"She must have slept off after binging on food and TV," he mumbled.

Vivek stretched out his hand in the dark to switch on the light. As he turned it on, the whole living room was flooded with colourful lights. With it came the music, a dance number from a 90s Bollywood film. He was stunned.

And then Antara came out, wearing a short dress and high heels. She sashayed and moved her body like how those item girls do in Bollywood songs, complete with pelvic thrusts and chest movements to try and seduce the hero.

Antara performed as she had practised, jiggling around Vivek, at times winking and pouting. She planted a loud kiss on Vivek's lips as the song finished.

"What's all this?" asked Vivek.

"Well, this is life. Fun. We can be happy," said Antara.

"We are fine together, Antara. There is no need for all this drama."

Antara stood close to him, looking into his eyes, and in a husky voice, said, "But I want more. Didn't you like my act?"

"It was the performance of a lifetime. Ladies and Gentlemen, the Oscar for best actor, female, goes to Antara, Antara Sachdeva. I'm really not in the mood for this, Antara, whatever this is..."

But Antara was undeterred. She took Vivek's hand.

"Come on, Vivek. Where is your sense of fun? There was a time when you would welcome this. I just want you to see that the old Antara is here. I am more than a housewife...more than a wife, more than a partner. I want you to see me...be with me." She unbuttoned his shirt, even as she reached up to kiss him on his lips. "There's more..."

Antara opened the bedroom door. The entire bed was covered with rose petals. She pulled her hair to one side and touched her lips with her fingers and ran her hands down to her breasts. "Perfect, isn't it?"

Vivek smiled. "You are being very filmy today. *Kya baat hai*?"

Antara smiled seductively, as she pulled the zipper on her dress. With measured movements, she shrugged off her dress, revealing sexy lingerie underneath. She reached for his trousers, drew down the zip and reached inside.

"Antara, what are you doing! I don't want to..." Vivek trailed off. His voice got huskier with every word.

"Oh?" said Antara with a grin, leaning forward.

Vivek groaned and his head fell back. A little while later, he bent and raised Antara's head, kissing her roughly. Soon, he forgot about his long and tiring day and his irritation, as he lay next to Antara making love.

12

Vivek had been following Leena wherever he could. He found out that Leena was summoned to the nearest police station and rushed there with his team of reporters. Leena quietly stepped out with her guards and sped away in her newly acquired Jaguar.

Vivek knew that he couldn't rely on his young and inexperienced reporters. This was a story meant for him and he'd confront Leena and get the truth from her.

In the last few days, Vivek had done extensive research on her life, her days as a small-time model and actress, her many flings with film directors and actors, her meeting with Amrit Shah and her marriage.

Without an interview in person, the whole story was pointless.

People had developed a soft spot for her as many news channels reported her as a victim of domestic abuse and applauded how she had emerged as the CEO of Lotus Enterprises. In fact, she had already appeared on the cover of three magazines and had bright chances of being awarded the *Woman of the Year* title.

He got to know that Leena was shooting a music video with her new IPL team in Film City. He barged onto the sets, calling out to Leena to come clean and talk to him. Leena didn't even look at him. He was tackled by her huge bodyguards and thrown out.

Later in the night, Vivek found his way through a toilet window into a posh night club in Bandra where Leena had thrown a party for her cricket team. All of Bollywood was there. The latest item girl was performing her hot new dance number. Vivek quietly walked past the crowd of glitterati and stood face-to-face with Leena.

Before the guards could pounce on him, he told her, "I know everything about you. Only a few years back you were a small-time model who hardly earned thirty thousand rupees a month. I know the names of each and every actor and director you have slept with. I know you met your late husband at a party and the moment you got to know that he owned a business worth ten thousand crore you hooked up with him. Amrit was already married with two daughters and you got him to divorce his first wife and got married to him. Your only aim was to have an easy, luxurious lifestyle. And then you killed him to take over his business."

By this time her guards had recognized and grabbed him. "I'm not going to let you get away like this," shouted Vivek.

The guests stared as he flailed his arms and legs, trying to pull away from the guards.

Leena smiled and shook her head. "Sorry, another stalker."

The next day, Vivek was summoned by the police commissioner and given a strict warning to keep away from Leena. "You are a senior journalist. I never expected this from you, Vivek. All those Bollywood people are laughing at you, calling you a stalker. If you are found stepping out of line again, you will be arrested. I hope I'm clear."

Vivek nodded and walked out. He knew

Leena had become too powerful. She was the new businesswoman and everyone wanted to be in her good graces.

Vivek decided to work on Saturday too. By midnight, he was mentally and physically exhausted. He walked out for a smoke, but his mind was racing to devise ways to get an exclusive interview with Leena. He knew none would work.

What would work for him was rest and lots of it before he took his next step.

He went home and slept. By the time he woke up, it was 11 a.m. Luckily, it was a Sunday.

Antara gave him tea and toast. He smiled. "I kept sleeping."

"It's good for you," she said. "The way you work, you need rest or you will crash."

He picked up the newspaper to see a large picture of Leena introducing her new range of cosmetics and threw it away. "This woman is the biggest fraud I have come across in my life. I'm going to expose her."

Antara picked up the newspaper and recognized Leena. "This is the same woman whose husband died by suicide, right?"

"He didn't die by suicide. She killed him. It was all planned by this Leena. She killed him to take over his business."

"I read in newspapers that her husband used to beat her and that day too she was beaten," said Antara.

"I knew Amrit Shah for many years. He was a true businessman who loved wine, women, world and wealth. He would never kill himself. This woman planned it in such a way that it looks like a suicide. She only had a few bruises on her body," said Vivek.

Antara didn't know what to say; she was the one who had killed him not Leena. "But I read that Amrit was drunk and high on drugs."

Vivek laughed, "It's not difficult for a beautiful woman to get a man high on drinks and drugs. And that's exactly what I'm going to prove. I'll peel off the layers of this mystery and expose this devil that killed Amrit."

Antara was happy that at least they were sitting and talking after a long time. At the same time, she was fearful of what would happen if Vivek ever got to know that she had killed Amrit and was the reason for another man getting electrocuted. Well, the second one survived, losing his right hand and his speech. He would never abuse again. The state government compensated his family with fifteen lakh rupees for their negligence that resulted in the accident.

All in all, a good job done by Antara.

Vivek got up and walked towards the bathroom. "I'm going for a bath. Let's have those onion and paneer parathas today."

"Sure," Antara smiled.

Earlier, Vivek would eat five or six of her parathas but now they survived on bread and sandwich spreads. She enthusiastically started to prepare the stuffing for the parathas.

Suddenly, her life was filled with excitement, love and adventure, and she felt productive. She had a new-found purpose in her life.

13

Through the day Antara busied herself with household chores, supervising the maids in cleaning the house, dusting, washing utensils and chopping vegetables. Once the work was done, she had a long bath and tried on various dresses. She settled on wearing Vivek's t-shirt and nothing underneath it. She felt free and happy. After a long time, they both seemed to have started to talk again, discuss, express their emotions and even laugh.

At 3.30 p.m., she switched on the TV to watch her favourite astrologer, Pandit Shiv Shambhu Pandey, talk about the effect of planets and reading out the horoscope for the day. As per Pandey ji, her fortune and good luck was seventy per cent. Not bad.

She went to sleep with a peaceful mind. By the time she woke up, it was already evening. She checked her phone to read the message from Vivek – Will be late.

She decided to go for a walk and changed into a kurta and leggings. She usually stepped out into the society after dark, to avoid other women. She started at a leisurely pace but then decided to make it a brisk walk. She had not even completed one round when one of the elderly women, Shagun Tripathi, called out, "*Arey*, Antara, where are you running away?"

Antara stopped and walked up to her, "Namaste, aunty."

"This is not right. Nowadays you don't even come for Tambola or bhajans. You have forgotten your aunty," Shagunji complained.

"No, aunty, you are my favourite. I've just been a bit busy with things."

"Haan, I know you are doing that IVF treatment. I have heard one has to take many injections. It must be really painful."

Antara quietly nodded.

"You shouldn't be doing this fast walk. Whenever I see you, I thank God that I didn't have to go through all this IVF treatment.

You know I have three sons and they are all settled in the US. Maybe next year I'll go to the US. See, this is real bliss, to be with your kids."

"Yes, aunty, I know. You are so lucky to have three sons in the US. They have been settled there for more than twelve years but you have not seen them or gone to the US at all." Antara forced a smile and replied sarcastically.

Shagunji gave a hollow laugh. "Their lifestyle is different. I cannot adjust in the US. I love my India. Okay, I have to go now. You better come to the bhajan party."

Antara smiled. She knew she had touched a nerve with the woman and was happy to have given her a dose of her own medicine.

Filled with determination, Antara completed five brisk rounds. She felt good. She had a light dinner and kept food for Vivek. She turned on the TV to watch a dance reality show but soon got bored and tuned into an old romantic movie instead. Nothing seemed to excite her. She turned off the TV and just sat there on the sofa. She closed her eyes and in an instant her soul was out of the body. Her body looked serene, almost sleeping peacefully.

She stood on top of a multi-storey building and hopped from one building to the other. This was fun.

Antara felt most alive in her soul form. It was the middle of the night and the streets were deserted.

Antara loved the way Mumbai glittered at night. It was good to be out of her drab housing society in an unknown suburban corner of the city.

She moved into dark and deserted alleys and zipped from one to the other like lightning.

She saw a refrigeration truck parked on the side on an alley. There were five men pushing teenage girls inside.

One of the men shouted, "Keep the temperature normal. I don't want the girls to freeze to death. Each of them will get us fifty thousand rupees."

The other three were forcing the girls to step inside. One of the girls resisted and was slapped and beaten.

Antara stood there watching. For a moment she felt helpless, trying to shout and stop the men.

Then she turned to the man who looked like their leader. She walked up to him and entered his body. The man's eyes gleamed with intent as he turned to his men, shouting at them to hurry. He walked up to them and started punching them and beating them. The men were stunned.

With this turn of events, Antara moved out of the gang leader and entered another man's body and he, in turn, started hitting the rest. The men seemed startled. Meanwhile, Antara slipped into the third man's body and he picked up an iron rod and started beating the others mercilessly. The men ran away, cursing him.

The man, whose body was under Antara's control, locked the truck door and drove it inside a police station compound. As the policemen ran out and started shouting at him, he stepped out, still possessed by Antara, and said, "There are girls inside the truck that we were planning to sell in Goa. There were four other men with me who ran away, but I'll give you all their details." He walked behind the truck and opened the door. The girls were crying.

The vehicle was impounded by the police. The girls were rescued and lady police officers were called in to help them. The man blurted out the details of his gang. With that, Antara moved out and vanished.

Suddenly, the man came back to his senses and realised he was in a police station. "Why have you picked me up? I have done nothing," he shouted.

The police were stunned. The man got up to run out but one of the policemen gave him a kick in the back and he fell face down on the floor.

Antara walked back and into her body lying on the sofa in her living room. She could hear some noises in the kitchen. Nervous, she tiptoed towards the kitchen and saw Vivek trying to make tea.

"What the hell happened to you? I have been trying to wake you up, but you seemed to be in a deep sleep, snoring away," he turned towards her and said.

Antara was quiet. She didn't know what to say.

Vivek smiled at her, "It's okay. Even I fall off to sleep like this. I didn't want to disturb you, so I thought I'd try my hand at tea."

Antara took a sigh of relief. "I had gone

for a brisk walk and took five rounds of the society. Maybe I overdid it and got a little too tired. You change and I'll get your tea."

Vivek smiled and walked out of the kitchen. "Thanks. It's been a long and hectic day. By the way, I'm going after that Leena and will prove that she is the one who killed her husband."

14

Leena had been flying all across the country, hobnobbing with the top political and corporate brass. She also brought in her closest school friend, Manpreet Brar, to be her personal assistant, giving her a fat salary and a luxury car. Both were seen together in almost all meetings, parties, and even in most pictures published in the media. There were talks that Manpreet was Leena's lesbian partner and both had planned this for a long time.

However, nothing seemed to affect Leena. She worked with a single-minded focus, almost monomaniacally, to strengthen her business by bringing in more investors, political masters and lobbyists under her umbrella. In spite of her busy schedule, she was always dressed in the best of haute couture. She had the best international designers designing for her. She was the toast of the town and she stood out among the pot-bellied corporate men.

The board of directors had started talking. "When does she sleep?" She is in Hong Kong at night, in morning she is calling from Tokyo. The share price of Lotus Enterprises had jumped ten times since she took over. She didn't live in Amrit's lavish fiftieth-floor apartment in Alta Mount Towers anymore. She had bought a sprawling bungalow in Juhu from a yesteryear Bollywood superstar and the bungalow's interiors were done by the star wife of a reigning superstar.

It was after two weeks of jet-setting across the world that Leena finally got to spend a night at her newly renovated bungalow. Late in the night around 12.30 a.m., she finished her calls and Manpreet handed her a glass of Scotch that Leena had taken to recently to calm her nerves. They raised their glasses and clinked to life.

Leena took a sip and swirled the Scotch in her mouth, tasting the bitter-sweet taste before letting it slide down her throat. "You know, I have never kissed a woman," she said to Manpreet.

Manpreet laughed. "I can understand why the whole country thinks we are some sort of lesbian partners."

"I still wish I had someone to love, to kiss, to make love to and come home to. We come home to all these gadgets, designs, furniture and luxury," sighed Leena.

"Now you are getting high, Leena. You are the hottest businesswoman this country has ever had."

Leena chuckled and did a bottoms up.

"Do we live to work or work to live?" Leena asked.

Manpreet smiled. "I can see the Scotch is working. Someone is getting all philosophical."

Antara, in her spirit form, stood on the side watching them, listening to their conversation. She wanted to confirm whether Leena was really a gold digger like Vivek believed. She seemed to be a normal girl inside, but greed had many forms. She wanted to find the truth.

Antara walked close to Manpreet and

touched her and, in an instant, took over. Her eyes lit up. She made another drink and handed it to Leena.

Antara, in Manpreet's form, sat close to Leena and held her hand. "Leena, we are best friends and you know everything about me. Still, you never told me about what happened between you and Amrit. I don't believe what many newspapers have written about you being a gold digger."

Leena gulped the drink in one go and kept aside the glass. "It's not that I loved Amrit, but I liked him. He was an ugly, fat guy who could make a woman laugh and one could talk to for hours. I liked that about him. I had not seen this quality in most men I met. Everyone wanted to sleep with me and then was gone. He was different. Yes, he was rich so it was a deadly combination. There's nothing wrong if a woman wants to marry a rich guy. I was not doing well in my career as an actress and I wanted a good life. I didn't rob anyone. I didn't force Amrit to marry me. He loved me and I enjoyed his company."

Antara was getting restless as Leena dragged her sentences and slurred. "You told the media and police that he used to beat you?"

"Yes, it started almost ten months after the marriage. His big financial deal didn't come through and he owed people huge amounts of money. He was always angry and started to drink and do drugs. He once whipped me with his belt. He had beaten me with his shoe for no reason many times. Then he started making demands that I sleep with other men to get him a lucrative deal or with his creditors so they wave off the loan. When I refused, he started threatening to kill me and throw me down from the fiftieth floor. Somewhere during our last argument, I fell unconscious and have no idea what happened afterwards," said Leena, laying down on the couch and closing her eyes.

With that, Antara stepped out of Manpreet's body and tumbled, asleep, on the couch.

Antara was now confident that Leena was not a bad girl. She had taken a lot of crap from Amrit in an attempt to take his business to new heights with her hard work, will, grit and passion.

She looked at herself in a salwar-suit, the *chunri* draped around her, and smiled, thinking. *"I'm just a housewife and will always remain so. Leena is fighting the male-dominated corporate and political world on a daily basis and flying high. I wish I could be someone like her or do what she is doing."*

She thought of Vivek who was desperate to prove that Leena had planned her husband's murder for the business. She looked at the lavish living room and expensive objects and antiques she had never seen before. She looked through a large glass window to see someone climbing down the wall into the bungalow compound. She hurried close to the wall to see it was Vivek, walking cautiously inside.

"Damn, he must have come here to confront Leena and get her interview on tape," thought Antara. She wanted to stop him somehow. She turned to look at both the women sleeping on the couch with their heads close to each other and their legs entwined. Anyone seeing them would assume that they were, lesbians.

She saw Vivek tiptoeing through the lawn towards the main building and suddenly sirens went off all over the place. He seemed to have stepped on something or tripped a wire. He forgot he was trespassing on the grounds of one of the smartest businesswomen of the country.

In a matter of seconds, the security guards were all over him. They recognized him and restrained him with plastic cords. His camera was taken away. The police were called, and he was handed over to them.

Antara stood there helplessly, seeing her husband being taken away in the police jeep.

15

Vivek was put inside the lock-up. He kept yelling at the inspector that all this had been made up by that Leena. "She's the real culprit. I'm going to bring out the truth and tell the world about her real face."

The policemen didn't give a damn. They were high on the liquor they got free every night from the many bars and restaurants they had inspected.

Antara stood inside the lock-up, watching Vivek pace up and down. He was tense and felt humiliated at the same time. As an assistant editor of a news channel, he understood its implications. If the complaint reached the higher ups in the media group, he could lose his job. If Leena spoke to other media channels and newspapers about him, he could lose his reputation. He shook his head and sat down in one corner. He vowed to expose Leena at any cost.

Antara felt helpless at his state. By now she knew a lot about Leena. She also knew that Leena hadn't killed her husband. What if someday Vivek found out that Antara was Amrit's killer?

The drunken police inspector, Pratap Shinde, walked to the lock-up and shouted at Vivek, "*Ae* you media, *saala*, you reporter type talk all nonsense about police and then you act so pricey as if you are some minister. Now I can break your legs right here, beat you black and blue and there won't be anyone to question me. *Behenchod*, you media people, you fabricate stories and think that you'll get away with it. *Saala chutiya*, you have been after that madam and I'm going to straighten you."

The inspector picked up a long fibre-glass stick. The newly issued ones used by the police now. He opened the lock-up and stepped inside, looking at Vivek. "Show me your media power now, *behenchod*. This is the police station. I'll show you my power."

Hawaldaar Bhonsle cut him off. "What the hell are you doing? If he gets hurt, the entire media will be after us. All our jobs will be in trouble. Get him out of there."

The inspector looked at him and shouted, "*Bhonsle behenchod*, you are a *randi, saala*. You are sold off to these media people. You love to see yourself on television. You think he's going to make you into a hero?"

With that the inspector swung the stick and it hit the wall. "So you are going to run away from me. I'm going to make you sit on this stick and make you dance." He swung the stick again.

Vivek shouted at the hawaldaar, "You better get him out of here. If this stick hits me even once, you know the entire media, be it newspapers or television channels, will come gunning after you and the entire police department."

Bhonsle understood the implications of raising one's hands on a media person and he walked in and pulled Inspector Shinde out. "Don't lose your strength over him. Your girl is here."

Hearing this, Shinde walked out, abusing Vivek and the media some more.

The police constables had brought a teenage beggar girl sleeping on the pavement for Shinde to shag off his demons. Shinde looked at her and pinched her bottom.

"Let me hear your cry," he said. The girl cried out and Shinde smiled.

Vivek shouted at him not to touch the girl or he'd report him. Shinde rotated the stick in his hand. "You refused the stick, so now she will get it."

Shinde took the girl inside a room at the back of the police station.

Vivek crouched against the wall, feeling helpless. He knew he would never be able to trace the girl among thousands of vagabonds in Mumbai, and even if he did, she would never testify against the inspector.

Inspector Pratap Shinde pushed the girl inside the room. "Tonight you are my bitch." He started to remove his uniform. The girl, crying, cowered in fear. Antara stood in front of her, watching them.

The girl tried to get up. The inspector pushed her down. It was then that Antara entered the girl's body. When the inspector again raised his hand, she grabbed it. Twisting it, she threw him down on the broken, cemented floor. The girl, with her eyes shining bright, looked around the room. She saw a fruit knife on a table. She extended her hand and grabbed the knife.

Antara's soul was filled with rage as she saw it all through the eyes of the girl. She pinned the inspector down on the floor, keeping her knee on his chest. With that, she started to cut his face with the knife. The inspector groaned and cried.

Those present in the police station thought that Shinde was making sounds of sexual gratification.

Vivek cried and kicked the wall in vain, shouting at them to help the girl. The policemen sat quietly, talking amongst themselves, passing lewd comments about Shinde's appetite and taking long gulps of their liquor.

The girl finished carving his face, writing "I AM A RAPIST" all over his face. The inspector had lost consciousness.

The girl wiped her blood-soaked hands on a towel kept in the room. She threw it over the inspector and walked out. She seemed to be in a trance. As she entered the front room of the police station, the hawaldaar looked at her and shouted, "Hey, done already?"

The girl didn't reply, kept walking, and moved out of the door.

The hawaldaar was stunned. "This Shinde must have fallen unconscious. Bloody bastard, the amount he drinks could make an elephant lose his consciousness."

The man walked up to the lock-up and opened it. "Sa'ab, you are a reporter and you understand these things. That Inspector Shinde gets mad once he drinks. See, we have not written any report against you. I request you not to report against us."

Vivek nodded and the hawaldaar let him walk away. "Don't worry about Shinde. Once he gets up in the morning, he'll be fine."

Vivek walked out of the police station.

Inspector Shinde was still sprawled on the floor inside the room with "I AM A RAPIST" tattooed in blood on his face.

Next morning, he was found by the area ACP. When questioned, everyone spoke up against Shinde to save their skin.

Shinde was dismissed immediately.

On his way home, Shinde got his entire face bandaged.

When his wife and daughter asked him what happened, he dismissed them casually. "It's just some cut. Don't bother me. I'm off duty for a few days, so I will rest at home."

The mother and daughter looked at each other. They preferred to leave him alone, lest he lose his temper.

His wife prepared *poha*, his favourite breakfast dish. Shinde had started to abhor his obese wife. He hated her presence around him when he had nubile girls to play with.

He would often shout at her, "You sit here all day and eat while I have to work all day and night. *Saala*, you housewives are useless. You make a plateful of *poha* and think your job is done."

This time he was quiet. He didn't say anything.

The wife walked in with a plate full of *poha* and kept it on a side table. She meekly said, "Please eat some *poha*. And...umm, I needed some money to buy the school uniform for Gayatri. She also needs a new school bag."

Last time she had asked for money, he had yelled at her. "I don't understand what you and your daughter do with all the money. *Saala*, you think I'm a *chutiya* sitting here. I know you both spend all my money on shopping, eating, and watching movies."

Today, Shinde told his wife to leave him alone and bolted the door from inside. He stood before the mirror and slowly started to remove the bandage. He saw the deep gash that read "I AM A RAPIST". He was stamped for life. He knew his past actions had caught up with him. Maybe this was karma or whatever they called it.

The suspended inspector put on his police uniform. He put on his brown shoes and picked up his service revolver. He checked it. It was loaded. He sat on a chair where his school-going daughter did her homework. He picked up a paper and started to write, confessing all his evil acts. He wrote that he took bribes, that he had raped many teenage girls and loved to beat them with a stick and that he was sick of it. Finally, he realised that he didn't deserve to live. He signed it with the date and time.

With that he took out the service revolver and put the nozzle right under his chin and shot himself.

The bullet smashed his jaw, travelling up through the nasal cavity, blowing away the cranium, splashing his brain matter all over the wall.

16

Antara was worried about Vivek. She didn't want him to lose his job over a sensational story. She could always talk to Leena and get him an interview and then he would be over this Leena case. It was a brilliant idea.

Leena was in Delhi meeting with the widows of the martyrs of the Indian Army as part of her philanthropic work. She gave a patriotic speech on the value of sacrifice, honour, and the respect that a soldier commanded. The widows had heard it many times. Many top corporate executives and Bollywood stars would come to meet them and use the event to promote their products, services, or movies. However, the widows received no help from any of them. The Bollywood stars would make the soldiers dance to their latest movie songs and at times distributed t-shirts, movie posters or organised a free screening. It was always about promotions and creating a brand of their own, never about the martyrs or their families.

The widows were pleasantly surprised when Leena announced that she'd be giving ten crore rupees for the welfare of the widows. No one had ever done that before. Manpreet was stunned. They had not planned on announcing anything like this. She kept signalling to Leena to cut short her speech and come down. In fact, Leena asked Manpreet to get the cheque book as she wanted to hand the cheque right there. Manpreet was left with no choice but to comply.

Leena wrote the cheque and handed it to Major General Rajeev Dhaiya, the chairman of the martyr's association. For the first time the women cheered for a guest and complimented her. Leena had no idea what had happened. It had been Antara's doing all the while and she felt overwhelmed with what she had achieved with this act. She knew it was a small sum for Leena and that she would generate another hundred crores in a few days. But for these widows, it could change their lives.

It was while they were going back to the hotel in their car that Manpreet shouted, "What happened to you? You just gave away a huge amount of money. Even five lakhs could have been good for them, but ten fucking crores. Are you out of your mind?"

Leena smiled at her. "Sometimes we need to share what we have. Don't worry, we'll make up for it." It was Antara talking, still.

Manpreet didn't understand what had happened to Leena. Leena had proven to be a pragmatic businesswoman who never gave in to such emotions. Suddenly she had become patriotic, talking about helping people and serving the nation, providing aid to soldiers and their families.

Leena took out her cell phone and dialled a number. "I know you have been dying to do a personal interview with me. Let's do it."

Manpreet turned to her, shell-shocked, "What the fuck? Who are you giving an interview to?"

Leena smiled. "It's that same reporter who has been following me and was arrested trying to barge into the house. I thought, let me be done with him. The more I delay it, the more they suspect and fabricate stories."

"Okay, let's keep it for tomorrow at my place, 10.30 in the morning. Don't be late or I might change my mind," said Leena, cutting the call.

17

The living room of Leena's bungalow had been turned into a studio. There were lights and cameras to cover every possible angle. Vivek was excited to be doing Leena's first exclusive interview since she took over as the CEO. He was dressed in a grey suit with a white shirt and black shoes.

The same guards stood all around the room. Vivek looked at them and smiled. "This time you can't throw me out. Your queen herself has called me to interview her."

Antara was happy to see a cheerful Vivek. Being his wife, she felt proud of him. The channel made sure that the interview was telecast live on national television. Their van was parked outside the bungalow with technicians working to get the show going. Antara made sure she remained in control of Leena till the interview.

Inside her room, Leena was dressed in her most exquisite diamonds and an outfit especially made for her by an Italian designer. She looked beautiful. Antara had grown slightly plump with round cheeks and some fat around her tummy. Even in her spirit form she felt conscious as Leena checked herself in the mirror.

In spite of her gruelling schedule, Leena took great care of her body with daily sessions of the gym, cardio and swimming. She had what they called the oomph factor of a seductress.

On the couch, Manpreet was going mad, giving her ready pointers on what to say and what not to. "He's here to grill you with his team. Don't give him anything to attack you with. He'll try his best to get you into a net with his volley of questions. Be very careful. It's going live, Leena. The whole country will be watching you."

"Isn't that wonderful? I get to say things in front of the whole country," smiled Leena.

Manpreet shook her head, "They are

going to start soon. We need to step out now."

Leena and Manpreet stepped out into her newly converted studio room. "Is this really my house?' said Leena. "You guys did a good job. I like the energy of this place."

Vivek stepped ahead and shook hands with her, "Hi! It's so good to finally meet you and interview you."

Leena looked at him with bright, shiny eyes, through Antara, and said, "Yes, finally, I get to meet you. It's good to see you smiling. Otherwise you seem to be a very serious bunch."

Vivek laughed. "Well, we'll see. I hope you are not scared."

"I live and dine with wolves every day," said Leena.

Vivek escorted her to the stage they had created with two big chairs facing each other. He helped her take the seat and said, "Be comfortable and take it easy. I'm here to talk about you and your life and your successes."

Leena smiled at him. "That sounds interesting. When do you start shooting?"

The producer started to give the

countdown as the whole team stood ready to go live. "4, 3, 2, 1... and, you are on, Vivek."

Vivek greeted and welcomed the viewers. He went straight to introducing Leena, the CEO of Lotus Enterprises, and, without losing any further time, dived into a question. "Did you kill your husband so that you could take over his business?"

Leena laughed. "You have been waiting to ask me this since my husband died. Sorry to disappoint you, but no, I did not kill him. The statement I gave to the police stands true and the police did their investigation and gave me a clean chit. It was a suicide."

Vivek looked at her with piercing eyes and asked, "You don't seem to miss him much with your luxurious lifestyle and jet-setting."

Antara took the opportunity to move out of Leena's body and let her do the talking. Her work was over. She wanted to do it for her husband, to see him smile, and to get him the exclusive he so desperately wanted. She did it like any good, obedient housewife would, if it were in her power to do so.

It came as a shock to Leena, as if she had come out of a coma. She looked around and started to shout, "What the hell is happening? How did I get here?"

Manpreet rushed towards her, whispering to her from the side, "You are live."

Leena took stock of the situation and straightened herself. She saw the many cameras and lights, and Vivek gawking at her.

"I'm sorry. It's just that I get disturbed whenever I'm asked these questions about my husband and his death. I'm just a woman and a wife at heart. I did my best to keep him happy, gave him all my love. I don't know what was going on in his mind. He seemed to be losing his mental balance and had started beating and abusing me. I never complained. After all, this is what girls are taught and trained from childhood; never to complain," Leena said. "Being a man, you'll never understand, but I know each and every woman watching me and listening to me understands and knows it in her heart. It's not easy being a wife, and that too a housewife."

Vivek knew Leena had just hit a six on the googly he tried to throw at her. With that she had also won the heart of all Indian women. "Have you thought of re-marriage or is there anyone in your life?" Vivek tried to throw a yorker instead.

She was not one to be scared or duck. She laughed. "There's no place for love, romance and marriage in my life. I'm only working and trying to help as many people as I can."

"Like you doled out a cheque of ten crore to the widows of the Indian Army soldiers?" said Vivek.

Leena was stunned and looked around for Manpreet. She had no clue that she had signed such a cheque. She controlled her emotions, and nodded, "Yes, anything for our soldiers and their families."

Vivek talked to her about business and her future plans and ended the show with, "I hope Leena will forgive me for stalking her everywhere to get an interview. Finally, she called me and agreed to do this."

Leena had no idea what he had said. She was surprised but smiled and gently nodded. "I realised you are an honest journalist who stands for the truth and fights the status quo. It was a pleasure meeting you and thank you for this interview."

With that the producer called cut. "Okay, we are done. Thank you everyone."

Leena got up and shot out from her chair and rushed inside her room followed by

Manpreet. Leena locked the door and said, "When did I sign that cheque? When did I agree to do this interview?"

Manpreet looked at her face blankly, "What's happening to you. I tried to tell you so many times not to do it, but you refused to listen. Anyway, it went well, and you were really good."

"Why don't I remember anything? Why would I give away such a big amount of money? You know me, Manpreet, and you didn't say anything," shouted Leena.

Manpreet looked at her worried, "I think you should see a doctor."

18

It was after months that they had come out shopping. Vivek got a day off post the exclusive interview that got the channel mega ratings. He was happy and talked about so many things. It was almost like Antara was seeing a totally new side of him. They held hands while walking through the crowded lanes and shared a plate of chaat-*paapdi*.

After months, Antara was smiling.

They chatted like they used to in the first few months of marriage. Vivek even bought her a little black dress, seeing which she shied away in embarrassment. "How am I supposed to wear that thing? All my fat will ooze out from all sides."

Vivek gently kissed her on the forehead. "You will look beautiful."

It was one of the rare moments of PDA; otherwise Vivek was always uptight about even holding hands or touching each other in public.

She wanted to buy new curtains and ordered a new coffee table. They ended up with loads of shopping bags and from there went for a movie.

To Antara it all felt like a movie. She pinched herself many times to make sure it was not a dream. She held on to Vivek like a child and didn't want to leave his hand.

Later in the evening, Vivek took her out to an Italian restaurant and they had pasta and red wine. She loved fine dining and it had been months since they had done something of this sort. It was heaven.

Vivek told her that he got an offer from another news channel to join as a senior editor. However, he felt that he was growing in his workplace and they now respected him for his work so he would prefer to stick with them. They finished one full bottle of wine between them and it gave her a beautiful fuzzy sensation.

"Why can't life be like this?" she thought.

In the night, they made love, and Antara was on the verge of tears. She kept her head on his shoulder and wrapped her legs around his. They talked some more and slept till late in the morning.

And it was a bright and happy morning. Antara prepared aloo parathas and even packed a few for him to share with his colleagues in the office. While leaving, Vivek said bye and kissed her on the cheek.

Antara started to make plans for the evening and made a list of things she wanted to buy for the house. She wanted to change the furniture and get a new dining table and sofa-set. She looked into her cupboard and threw out all her old salwar-suits and sarees.

She had forgotten about the little black dress Vivek bought her. She took it out and looked at it. Maybe this could be a surprise for Vivek in the evening. She hurriedly took off her clothes and somehow managed to slip into the dress. It hardly covered her 'thunder' thighs and showed her round and heavy shoulders and arms.

She was suddenly too conscious of her weight and looks. She thought of Leena, who looked stunning in the revealing dress she wore. Her arms, legs and shoulders were almost crafted to perfection like the designer dresses she wore.

Antara made a resolution to join a gym and start with regular exercises and turn the roly-poly housewife into sexy Antara.

19

Leena secretly got her medical exam done. She didn't want the media or her board of directors to find out about it. She got her entire body examined, right from CAT scan, MRI scan and everything possible to examine the brain, the neurons, the heart and all.

The doctors told her she was perfectly okay. At times such things happened due to stress and anxiety. They advised her to take it easy and go on a vacation and get loads of fresh air.

She decided to get out of Mumbai and away from the office to the farmhouse in Lonavala. The monsoons had just started, and the place was lush green. The hills looked beautiful with fresh grass and the air was clean. Leena had left Manpreet in Mumbai to take care of the day-to-day activities and to keep her informed. Also, she needed some time alone.

The first day she lounged around her farmhouse and looked at the many horses they had in the stables. She checked the backyard where they grew vegetables. Then she saw a few paragliders flying over the lake. She was tempted to fly, and finally in the evening, she reached the place.

On a hillock she met with Avi Malik, an ex-Indian Air Force pilot, the founder of Templepilots, the ace paraglider in the country. Avi taught her the basics and guided her in her first flight. It was breath-taking to fly above the waters of the lake by the setting sun and over the hills. She laughed and had a great time. It opened up many locked doors inside her heart. She felt lighter, breathed easier, felt more confident. After all, she could fly, and to her amazement, was singing.

She also met Jimmy Mistry, one of her foremost business rivals, who had also come to fly. They shook hands and Jimmy told her about his farmhouse, which happened to be close to Leena's farm. They promised not to talk business and only unwind from the daily stress and pressures.

As the moon rose over the hills, she walked bare feet with Jimmy, Avi and other flyers. She felt the wind in her face and the cool waters of the lake splashing on her legs. She had never done something like this before.

As darkness started to spread, she invited them over for dinner. The evening turned into a big party and Leena brought out the best wines from her collection and had top chefs from Mumbai plate amazing food. Jimmy brought his collection of Scotch. They drank and drank and drank. Jimmy, in spite of being a Parsi, turned out to be an encyclopaedia of old Hindi film songs. He won every round of antakshari they played.

By the time everyone left, it was 3 a.m. Leena walked into her bedroom and slept. She woke to check the time; it was 12.30 in the afternoon. She hurriedly jumped out of the bed but soon realised that she didn't have to go to office and had the luxury to laze around. She came out to a light drizzle. All around, the green grass and trees looked beautiful with sparkling new leaves. *"Can life really be so simple?"* she thought.

She tried to trace back the events of last evening and remembered each one. She didn't suffer from any memory loss. In fact, she hadn't done anything foolish like sign the cheque or call that Vivek fellow for an interview.

"How and why did I do that?" was a question she had not been able to answer.

Leena was not the kind to let go.

20

Antara sat in front of the television watching a news report by Vivek as he spoke about Subodh Nagarkar, the social welfare minister of state, who owned five sugar mills and projected himself as the champion of women's rights. Vivek was talking to him over the phone in a live report. "The committee of village women have reported that ten days back five of their female workers had gone to meet you but have not yet returned. There's no trace of them."

The minister chuckled, "You know I am always there for these women, but no one from the committee came to meet me or any of my workers. I have no idea about these women. It's a ploy by the Opposition to malign my name."

Vivek moved to another question. "What about accusations about hoarding sugar and grains?"

"The media has a lot of questions, so I am organising a press conference in the evening at my office. All media personnel are invited and I'll take all questions from you people and answer them in front of the whole nation. I hope that will satisfy you."

By 6 in the evening, the entire media had crowded outside the minister's office. There was heavy police deployment. Subodh Nagarkar was conducting a press conference after a long time, taking direct questions from the media. Many top police officials were there. Vivek was there with his team. Antara too stood there, quietly watching the proceedings.

The minister arrived with his guards and took his place behind the forest of mikes. He smiled at all the journalists, "Let's not waste any time and start straightaway."

A group of village women stood on the side protesting. One of the women shouted, "Five of our women have disappeared. They had come here to complain about the rising crime against women in the state and have not been seen since then. We fear they have been killed."

The minister folded his hands and, with a sombre face, said, "You all know I respect women and bow down to them. For me, all women are an incarnation of the Devi. However, I have no idea about these women that you are talking about."

Antara turned to see some little girls wailing in the group. Their mothers were missing. Antara decided then that everyone had the right to know the truth, what she had learned the previous evening when she had happened to visit the minister in her astral form and listened in on his instructions to hide the sacks and keep quiet about the women. "One peep out of you and you will meet the same end as them," he had said.

She entered the minister's body and his eyes turned bright.

Vivek got up to ask, "Sir, there are more than sixty women here who claim that those five women went to your house to meet with you. How can you deny this?"

The minister smiled and said, "I'm not denying it. Yes, those women did come to my bungalow with some reports and complaints. Well, my men were in the mood to have some fun, so they took those women inside. It seems the women died, and I was told that their bodies were cut into pieces and thrown into the sewers. You might still be able to find some body parts there."

The entire media, police officers, his staff and women were stunned to hear this. The people watching it on the TV were shocked. The officers on duty started making calls to their seniors to ascertain what to do in this situation.

The minister went on, "This is politics. A lot of things happen. I have five sugar mills and, yes, we do hoard a lot of sugar. Once the price rises, we release it. It's a simple and easy way to earn quick profits. If you don't believe me, you can go down into the basement of my bungalow. There's a secret vault inside the bathroom there and you'll find at least five hundred crore rupees in cash. See, I'm not a small fry."

The police commissioner issued immediate orders to arrest the minister. As he rattled on about his properties, the police officers on duty grabbed him and announced that they were taking him into custody.

Antara moved out of his body and stood away, watching.

The minister suddenly looked around and shouted, "What are you doing? You cannot arrest me. I will get all of you suspended." He had no clue of what had happened a while ago.

The minister was forced inside a police jeep and taken away. Antara smiled and saw Vivek standing there with a puzzled face.

Antara winked at him and smiled. *Dekha housewife ka kamaal.*

21

Antara was thrilled to be able to bring out the dirt of society and teach a lesson to some dirt bags. This was how it felt to be an empowered woman and that too with extraordinary powers. But she also wanted to be a perfect housewife and take care of her husband, her house, and hopefully become a mother one day. That would complete her family.

She was making Vivek's favourite vegetable, stuffed karela (bitter gourd). It took a lot of time to prepare, but Antara now enjoyed doing things for him. After all, things were changing. Her cell phone beeped and she saw a WhatsApp message from her mother. Rajshri had sent her a picture of her backless and sleeveless blouse. Antara was zapped and called her mother immediately.

"What are you wearing, Mummy? I mean, just look at it. It's backless and sleeveless. What's left of it?" said Antara.

Her mother laughed out. "I'm hot, not cold like you. *Arey*, you don't know how many men walk into my boutique to see me and wait to say namaste. I'm in demand, sweetheart."

Antara cut her off, "*Ae ki ho gaya hai aap ko*, don't forget you have a daughter, who's been married for over eleven years."

"That doesn't make me an old and boring person. I'm not like you. I want to live my life fully and filled with excitement. You are sitting there in Mumbai, the so-called big city, but what do you do? Nothing. You spend your whole day inside your flat."

Antara wanted to tell her all about her new-found powers and what all she had done. But she stopped herself. "I'm not boring. I have the responsibilities of a housewife."

The mother laughed. "Don't forget, you are a woman. Why do you wear those things? *Arey*, your mother runs the hottest boutique in Karol Bagh and you wear Lajpat Nagar-type suits."

"Okay, what do you want me to do?" asked Antara, getting irritated with her mother.

"First, you need to change yourself. I want you to go get a nice haircut, get some facial, pedicure and manicure done. You think you're a true housewife, but you don't understand these men. They like to see hot women. You have to get some sexy, short dresses and stuff your bra to make your boobs look big."

"Mummy, please!"

"*Arey tu chup kar*, I know these men inside out. Just follow my advice and see how your marriage starts to rock and roll. Another thing, change the interiors of your house. It doesn't look like a house anymore. It looks like a cheap hotel room. Go change your furniture, wall paint, gadgets and everything," said Rajshri with a big smile.

Antara was shocked and couldn't say anything.

"*Achha*, you better get working. I have to go for my golgappas and chaat. You know there's this retired colonel. He comes there whenever I'm there. I'm thinking of saying hi to him."

With that she cut the call and Antara stood there frozen, her mind whirling.

22

Antara got a new haircut from an expensive salon and a manicure and pedicure after months. She had always been trying to save up for something or someday and had forgotten to live her life.

Back home, she did her make-up, wore a sexy short dress, and put pads under her bra. She looked at herself in the mirror and laughed at how big she looked.

As always, Vivek returned around eleven. He stepped out of the groaning lift and rang the bell. There was no response. He waited and again rang the bell. Still, no answer.

"What's she up to now?" He took out his key and opened the door to step inside a dark house. He called out, "Antara, come out."

No response.

Out of habit, he extended his hand and pressed the switch and light filled the room. He saw the entire living room looked different. The walls were covered with wallpaper. There was a new sofa, a new dining table, a large-screen LED TV. There were paintings on the walls, expensive vases and other stuff.

"Antara, what's all this?" he shouted.

Music filled the air. Antara came out in a micro mini, gyrating to the number, and moved around him like a pole dancer straight out of a Bollywood item number.

Vivek looked at her and couldn't stop laughing.

"Is this our house?" he asked.

"Yes, I have changed everything," said Antara.

"Really, darling?"

Antara held his hand and took him into the kitchen, showing him the new refrigerator; microwave oven, mixer-grinder, coffee maker and a front-loading washing machine.

"Where did you get the money for all this?"

"I got it all on EMI. You can keep paying the monthly instalments," said Antara and gave him a kiss.

Vivek looked at her and said, "Did your mother tell you to do all this? I know she keeps giving you a lot of gyan on relationships."

"Why should my mother tell me everything? It was my idea. Do you like it?"

"Do I have a choice?" said Vivek. "I too have a surprise for you. We are going to Goa. My channel is paying for the trip."

Antara danced with joy.

The entire exposé of minister Nagarkar had been credited to Vivek, as he had been chasing him for months, coming out with many scams related to the man. Finally, it seemed the minister had cracked under the pressure, that too at his own press conference.

Vivek was rewarded with a three-night stay at Taj Exotica in Goa with his family.

23

Antara was feeling on top of the world. It had been years since they had a vacation and Goa turned out to be heaven. They soaked in the pool for hours and had drinks and talked till late in the night. She couldn't believe this was happening.

They rented a Scooty and Antara drove it, Vivek riding pillion. There was a time when she used to drive her Scooty in Delhi and had saved enough to buy her first car, but then she got married. It was like reliving those free and happy days on her beloved two-wheeler. They stopped at roadside cafes, went to beaches, and lounged around on the beach chairs, sipping beer, and only after they had watched the sun set together, hand-in-hand, that they returned to the hotel.

They gorged on the best food, wine, and had fantastic sex. In fact, Antara realised that they had not even switched on the TV. They would sit and talk for hours, discussing their life, dreams and their little world.

Vivek told her that as a reporter he couldn't go any higher than this, so maybe he should start focusing on having his own news channel. Antara was thrilled that she too could pitch in or get a job with him. They laughed and laughed. This is what they called being happy.

Antara spent one whole afternoon at the exotic spa getting all sorts of beauty massages and treatments. Everything was paid for by Vivek's organisation. Antara realised that maybe she was too harsh with him at times and got too cranky, doubting him for everything. Maybe she just needed to relax and learn to be happy. Even being happy had become a task.

Antara decided that she would change and have a more loving and accepting attitude towards Vivek. She had to understand the life and work of a television reporter and the stress that came with it. Suddenly, she was the most understanding wife in the world. *"If we are happy together, everything is justified,"* thought Antara and smiled to herself. It was more than happiness. It was bliss.

Later in the evening, they sang karaoke in the restaurant in front of all the guests who clapped and cheered for them. They kept it on with playing antakshari and Vivek belted out some of the oldest Hindi film songs that she had never heard before. In fact, she had never seen this side of Vivek. It was surprising and refreshing.

They had a Goan beach wedding and were congratulated by all the guests. Vivek even went ahead and ordered drinks for everyone. This was not covered under the paid trip. These were the moments when money didn't matter; it was love. It was love, pure and beautiful.

Antara felt like that young girl who fell in love at the first sight of Aamir Khan while watching his debut film, *Qayamat Se Qayamat Tak*. She was in a dream world and didn't want this trip to end.

Antara's spirit form had come to check on Leena and found that she too seemed to be happy with her break and was chilling at her farmhouse. Towards the evening, Leena decided to go riding to the other side of the lake to meet the paragliders.

She rode her favourite horse, Bolt, and took him out on a gentle trot. She had learnt the basics of horse riding at the Mahalakshmi Racecourse as Amrit had wanted her to be there at every derby race to mingle with the hotshots of the city. In fact, she had taken lovingly to the sport and started to communicate with horses and understood them quite well. She knew exactly what they loved and enjoyed, how to pat them and get them out for a gallop, trot, or canter.

She rode through the hills around her farm and, as she turned on a steep curve, she saw Jimmy Mistry on his horse, coming towards her. He waved at her and she gave him a nod. Jimmy rode up to her. "That's a nice horse. I hope you can ride that."

Leena smiled at him. "You want to bet. From this point to across the lake," she pointed to a wind sail placed by the Templepilots to guide their paragliders.

"I don't ride. I glide," said Jimmy and rode off. Leena laughed and caught up with him.

They rode almost neck to neck around the hill over the rocky path. "So, do you give up or are you still game?" Jimmy called out.

He gave her a mocking smile and sped ahead. Leena saw his horse galloping at full speed. She tried to catch up with him. Suddenly, at a turn, Jimmy and his horse both seem to have vanished. There was no sound of the hoofs too.

Leena stood there for a moment, staring ahead. She took out her mobile phone and called the police.

24

It was at the Goa airport, on their way back to Mumbai, that Vivek saw the news report about a freak horse-riding accident that had killed Jimmy Mistry.

It was Leena who had called the police. She had witnessed the accident and said, "We were racing, and he missed a sharp turn on the hill. By the time the horse could stop, they fell down into the deep ditch covered with rocks." A few locals who saw it corroborated Leena's version.

But Vivek realised that Jimmy Mistry was Leena's foremost business rival.

By the time the local police reached the spot, Jimmy's body was crushed between the rocks and the horse. The local police wrote it off as an accident. A few business channels talked about how it affected the share price of his company, but nothing much after that.

Vivek was sure that it was Leena who got him killed. The one and only business rival out of her way. He started investigating into it and got to know that Lotus Enterprises bought over 27 percent of Jimmy's company a day after his death. His suspicion was confirmed. He was sure that it was Leena who had killed her husband, and now Jimmy.

This was a very dangerous woman and could be the biggest story of his life.

One exclusive interview had turned him into a star. He could well imagine his bosses licking his feet once he exposed Leena and shattered the image of an empress that people had of her, and presented her as a cold-blooded killer. Maybe he would get some funders to open his own news channel. He was thrilled. He felt a new wave of energy rush through him. He knew she wouldn't let him get it all so easy. He was ready for the big fight.

He discussed his suspicions with Antara, trying his best to convince her that Leena was behind the deaths of Jimmy and her husband.

Antara didn't know how to clear his suspicions regarding Leena. She was happy that he was discussing things with her; otherwise he would come home and hit the bed. Nowadays, they sat together, shared a drink and talked or rather he talked and she gave him a good ear. All 'good' housewives are supposed to do that.

She made sure that she prepared all his favourite dishes, kept his shirt ironed, his shoes and socks ready and that he didn't forget his cell phone. She was happy doing these small things. At least there was harmony in the house. They talked and touched and laughed.

Antara waited for the weekend. She had started making plans for another shopping trip and movie. Late on Friday evening, Vivek told her that he was leaving for Lonavala to investigate the story and would be there for the next two days. She was left disappointed.

In Lonavala, Vivek met with the inspector who had investigated the death of Jimmy Mistry. He spoke to him at length, but the police had nothing new to tell him. He knew Leena was too smart to have left any evidence. She turned her husband's death into a suicide, Jimmy's into an accident.

He decided to go to the accident site and look for clues.

First, he went down to the bed of rocks where Jimmy had crashed with his horse. He could still see dried blood on the rocks. He looked around in the hope of finding some evidence. Nothing.

Antara had come to see him. She saw a man obsessed with a story, trying to prove it right. Vivek looked up at the point from where Jimmy had fallen onto the rocks. The place was high up on a hill. So he decided to walk all the way up, scouring the path, bushes and trees for some evidence.

He had forgotten to carry water and was sweating by the time he reached. He could see the sharp curve on the path from where Jimmy had fallen. It was clear from the police report that he seemed to be coming at high-speed and had failed to make the turn, resulting in the fall and death.

Vivek sat there at the tip of the curve, looking down at the rocks. It was the perfect way to an easy death.

"Could Leena have planned all of this?" he

thought. "She has proven to be a manipulative and calculative woman. She killed two men and took over their business to be the latest darling of the business world as well as the media. She must have studied the terrain, got Jimmy out for horse-riding, and lured him here."

Antara knew there was nothing to prove. Leena hadn't killed Jimmy.

Vivek looked around for footprints, but the rain had washed away everything. So he decided to go to Leena's farm and look around. Antara seemed to enjoy seeing him work like a detective, her own Sherlock Holmes. However, she wanted to laugh at his silly theories. But he was her husband. She ought to have had some respect for him and not mock him.

He walked through the hills and reached Leena's farm. There was a huge board outside that read 'Garden of Eden'. He almost laughed. He looked for a way to get in but the whole place was locked in by a high, cemented wall and barbed wires. He gathered some bricks and stood over them to climb the wall, ducking under the barbed wires before jumping inside.

Antara sat on the large swing and smiled at him. Vivek quietly moved around the place. He walked inside, looking into the rooms. He moved out and saw the stables. He moved towards them and saw many fine breeds of horses and mares.

A stable boy shouted at him, "How the hell did you get in?"

Vivek raised his hand and smiled. "Mumbai Police, we have a warrant to search this place. If you try to disrupt the work, you can be arrested."

The boy called out to the others and soon five men stood around Vivek. Somehow, he managed to stand his ground. Antara watched with amusement as he played the role of a Mumbai crime-branch officer. One of the stable heads wanted to make a call to Mumbai, but Vivek stopped him. "I'm here to talk to you guys, so don't try to act smart."

He looked at them and asked, "Tell me, where was Leena when Jimmy met with the accident?"

One of the boys almost spoke out, but the others gave him a stern look and he shut up.

"Well, I can take you to Mumbai and you all will be put in lock-up. Maybe there you'll talk," said Vivek.

The eldest one said, "Sa'ab, we are all simple workers who take care of the horses and the place. That day Leenaji went out riding on Bolt and came back after two hours. In fact, she herself called the police. It was an accident. There are so many sharp curves on the hills. Jimmy seemed to be overconfident about his riding skills, but a horse is an animal not a car that you can manoeuvre wherever you want."

Vivek quietly nodded, listening to the man. He walked inside the stables to have a look at the beautiful Bolt. The horse didn't allow him to come near him.

Vivek was happy with his work and moved out to check on Jimmy's farm that was adjacent.

25

It was simply called 'Mistry's Farm'. Antara was already inside, trying to help Vivek in his investigation. He sneaked in through a crack in the wall.

Mistry's Farm was an old, battered building with large lawns and old trees standing tall with their roots spread out. The stables were mere brick structures that housed his horses.

A few dogs barked and Vivek hid behind a tree, fearing they could be trained guard dogs. The dogs turned out to be stray ones who had sneaked through the broken wall. There were five dogs fighting amongst themselves at a patch on the ground.

Antara noticed that they were digging in the ground.

An old man tried to shoo them away, but the dogs were angry. They barked and almost attacked him. The old man backed away and went inside.

Vivek walked inside, following the old man and gave him the same story of being a crime-branch officer from Mumbai. He asked him several questions, but nothing seemed to point at Leena. He asked whether Leena came to their farm, but the old man said, "Never, I don't think Jimmy sa'ab even knew Leena."

Outside, the stray dogs had ripped apart the ground. Antara could see what the dogs were after. She wanted to shout out to Vivek and call him but couldn't. She wanted to bring their attention to the dogs and she saw the horses. She went and touched a horse. Soon, her spirit took over the big horse.

The horse broke through the stables and ran out neighing. The old man saw this and ran out. He saw the horse charging at the dogs. For a moment the dogs stood in rapt attention looking at the horse and then ran away.

The old man managed to grab the reins to take him back to the stable. "How did you manage to break the rail and jump out?"

The horse had never done that before.

Vivek was frozen to the spot. He saw a human hand sticking out of the ground where the dogs had been digging. He ran away and called the local police.

The police team brought two labourers and they dug around the land. Soon they discovered two female bodies. One was of an adult and the other looked like that of a teenager. The old man was called to see whether he recognized any of them. He saw them and cried out, "It's Mistry madam, Jimmy sa'ab's wife, and their daughter."

Vivek knew he had hit upon a big story. He called up the chief editor and updated him on the developments. He wanted to report live and a van was dispatched to Lonavala. He could see that the bodies were not fully decomposed. He asked the old man, "Who did this? They were missing for many days and you didn't even notice?"

The old man had teary eyes. "I have no idea. Yes, they came with Jimmy sa'ab and I never saw them after sa'ab's accident. I thought they had gone back to Mumbai."

Slowly, things were unravelling in front of Vivek. He never saw Jimmy's wife and daughter during his last rites. Jimmy's brother and his family were there, but his wife and daughter weren't. He was told the daughter and wife were in shock and too shaken up to be present at the funeral.

"Could it be possible that Jimmy's family was killed by his brother?" thought Vivek. *"Then they would have killed Jimmy too. Why turn his death into an accident and bury his wife and daughter?"*

He knew anything was possible. People committed heinous crimes for money, power and lust. In this case, it was clear to him, it was Jimmy's business and properties. Once his family was gone, there was no one left to make a claim. It had to be Jimmy's brother.

Meanwhile, Antara was doing her own investigation. She entered a stable boy who opened the large wooden doors of the old garage. Vivek saw the doors opening as they creaked and swung out. He could see an old Mercedes car parked inside. Near the wall were piles of tools and toolboxes.

The stable boy opened the boot of the car and the sound attracted Vivek. The boy took out a cloth and started to clean the car. Vivek walked closer to the boot and opened it to see a shovel, a big hammer and a pile of clothes soiled in blood. He called out to the police.

The clothes, the hammer and the shovel along with other tools were taken away by the police to be sent for a forensic examination in Mumbai. Antara moved out of the stable boy. He had no idea what had happened. He told the police that the car remained in the garage and was taken out only when Jimmy sa'ab came.

By the afternoon, Vivek was live on his news channel reporting from Lonavala, describing in detail the discovery of the two bodies, the murder weapons, and the clothes of the murderer from Jimmy's farm.

The channel ratings skyrocketed.

Antara knew that none of them knew anything, yet.

26

It had been one of those days when Antara was bored sitting alone in the house. She decided to roam the city.

Antara was attracted to a new high-rise near Mahalakshmi, where each flat was worth over thirty-five crore rupees. At times she tried to imagine all the 500-rupee notes that would equal to such a huge amount. She was curious about the people who lived in such expensive homes.

She had found most people living there to be exactly the same as others – insecure, scared, uncertain, unloved, deceitful, cheats and frauds; houses where domestic violence, rapes and murders were as common as in the slums.

She walked through various apartments until she reached the penthouse where she had seen Jimmy Mistry shouting at and abusing his wife. When a young teenage girl tried to intervene, Jimmy had slapped her hard. At this, his wife had charged at Jimmy, trying to hit him with both hands, but the man pushed her away, shouting, "I told you I want a divorce. I can't live with you anymore."

"If you want a divorce, go file for one. But I'll make sure you give me and my daughter more than half of your business and property. I'm not going to let you get away so easily. I have had enough of your abuse and beatings."

The daughter had hugged her, crying. "You want your share in the business and property, you'll get it," Jimmy had said and stormed out.

Antara had kept a close tab on Jimmy ever since, following him from his house to his office to his mistress, a young Bollywood starlet.

Antara remembered Jimmy telling his mistress that he planned to get away from his wife permanently. From that day Jimmy mostly behaved around his wife and daughter. He didn't file for a divorce. He turned into a good father and brought gifts for his daughter. The arguments stopped.

Then one day, out of the blue, he invited them to the Mistry farm in Lonavala. Both the wife and daughter were excited that the family was getting back together. Antara had no idea of Jimmy's plan and could never have imagined that a father was capable of what he did.

Jimmy had taken both women to their farm and they had spent three happy days together. They were a unit, giving all the appearance of happiness. Then Jimmy Mistry gave the whole staff two days off so that the family could have some privacy and spend quality time together.

Late one night, Jimmy got drunk, picked up a big hammer, and beat his wife and daughter to death. He brought out a shovel, dug a deep pit inside the farm, and buried them there.

Antara, meanwhile, was excited about her relationship improving with Vivek and had almost forgotten about Jimmy. That night, while they were still in Goa, she had decided to visit Jimmy and saw him burying the mother-daughter duo. She was shaken up. So, this was what he had meant by getting away from them permanently. He had killed them mercilessly and buried them. Antara was shattered at the gruesome act.

She decided not to let Jimmy walk away so easily. She took over him, and in that possessed state, made him put the blood-soaked hammer, shovel and clothes inside the garage. She made him write a note and put it inside the pocket of his bloodied trousers.

For two days Jimmy was alone at his farmhouse. He indulged in paragliding and horse riding. He even met Leena, his business rival. They were galloping around the hill and near a steep curve when Antara entered the horse and the horse spooked. She made sure that the horse ran and jumped to their death over a bed of rocks.

Antara wanted Jimmy to feel the pain, the danger, his life ebbing away bit by bit, and stare death in the face. She made sure that he fell on the sharpest of rocks with the entire weight of the horse crushing him. She wanted him to feel his skull crack and split open like the blows of the hammer that he used on his wife.

Jimmy, the wife-beater, cheater and murderer, was dead. And Leena, the innocent bystander in the incident, had called the police.

Upon returning from Goa, Antara sat on the sofa, mulling her actions. She was clear about one thing—all men deserved what they got.

She knew that her Vivek was not an idiot, that he would have put two and two together.

"Should I tell him the truth before he finds out?" she wondered.

27

Early in the morning, Leena was in her office when Manpreet rushed in and switched on the large flat-screen television. "Have you heard this?"

Vivek appeared onscreen, showing a few pages of the forensic report. "Our channel was the first to report on Jimmy Mistry's death and the more mysterious deaths of his wife and daughter. We have with us the forensic report that declares that it was Jimmy Mistry who killed both his wife and daughter."

Leena and Manpreet were stunned.

"What the hell? Why did he kill his own daughter and wife?" said Leena.

"The forensic report clearly states that the fingerprints found on the shovel and hammer used in killing and burying the bodies were of Jimmy Mistry. Also, the blood stains found on the clothes were that of his wife and daughter. The forensic lab has also found traces of Jimmy's DNA on the clothes. The report says that Jimmy killed them with repeated blows on the head with the hammer and then buried them inside the farmhouse."

"How could he do that?' said Manpreet. "This is inhuman."

Vivek took out a piece of paper and the camera zoomed in on it. "Here's a copy of the handwritten letter that was found inside Jimmy's garage. The forensic lab has verified the handwriting. It belongs to Jimmy Mistry. This was Jimmy's last note before his death. I'll read it for you. Actually, it's a suicide note."

Leena and Manpreet looked at each other. They were both confused and puzzled.

"I hereby confess that I have been addicted to various drugs and got into many affairs with various women. Throughout all this, I totally neglected my wife and daughter. Recently, I was involved in an affair with a young woman and wanted to marry her. My wife refused to divorce me and my daughter stood by her side. They even threatened to take a substantial part of my properties and business if I filed for divorce. In my greed and lust, I killed them and buried them in the farmhouse. I have realised that I have committed a ghastly sin. My only redemption is in my death. I hope God will forgive me."

The camera zoomed closer on the name signed under it. "You can look here. The name signed is that of Jimmy Mistry. Well, we found the killer but sadly he took his own life. He knew of the sharp curve and deliberately made the horse run and they both fell to their death. Case closed."

Leena was relieved. "Thank God, it was death by suicide and my name was not dragged into it."

"It's all clear. I hope he gets clarity in his head and stops bothering you," said Manpreet.

But Vivek was far from getting some sort of clarity as he came out after the news bulletin. He sat outside, smoking and sipping hot tea. "First, Amrit Shah died by suicide. Then a police inspector was branded with "I AM A RAPIST" and he too died by suicide. Then Nagarkar rattled out the truth in front of national media. It was suicide. And now Jimmy Mistry jumps to his death with his horse? Another suicide and a note left behind. Could there be a connection, or am I just reading too much into this?"

He started to make pointers on a note pad and remembered the incident about the traffickers who fought amongst themselves. One of them drove the girls inside the truck to the police station and later didn't seem to remember anything. Even Leena was unconscious when her husband jumped and later didn't remember much.

He realised all these men, dead or punished, were evil men, who had committed evil deeds.

"Is there a vigilante targeting evil doers or is something else going on?"

He decided he must solve the mystery.

28

The 9 p.m. show ran a full story on the spate of recent deaths by suicide that included prominent businessmen Amrit Shah, Jimmy Mistry, and the police inspector. Vivek also called in a panel of experts. The psychologists theorised that stress and anxiety levels had peaked so high that people were not able to cope with the smallest of failures or challenges. The policemen were obviously overworked, underpaid and stressed. There were many instances where CRPF men and other paramilitary soldiers had shot their senior officers and then killed themselves.

Vivek had also invited Leena to be a part of the discussion but she never responded.

She didn't want to rake up the past and preferred to forget the dead.

Antara saw the media and experts dismissing them all as suicides. She realised that all these deaths had really amounted to nothing. She couldn't keep scouring the whole city for such scum and killing them. This would never end.

Antara finally realised the hopelessness of it all and decided that prevention was always better than the cure. She decided to issue a warning.

She walked out of her house and took an auto-rickshaw to the Goregaon station and went to a phonebooth nearby. It was hard to find phonebooths nowadays. From there she called Vivek on his cell phone, talking in a heavy-accented voice with some tissues over her mouth.

Vivek had just come out of the studio after wrapping up the 9 p.m. show. She told him that all these suicides were not suicides but murders and that she had also made the state minister Subodh Nagarkar confess to his crimes.

"Who's this? What nonsense are you talking?" shouted Vivek.

"I'm telling you the truth. All these men were killed."

"How can you say that?" he asked.

"Because I did it," said Antara.

Vivek fumbled for words and Antara continued, "All the men wronged women. They were wife-beaters, cheaters, rapists and murderers. I killed them and made it all look like an accident or suicide. In case of the police inspector, I wrote "I AM A RAPIST" on his face. That drove him to die by suicide. Finally, he understood the shame that rape victims have to live with."

"Who are you?" Vivek said.

Antara calmly said, "I'm a housewife and I would like to warn all men who ill-treat women, especially rapists, wife-beaters and cheaters. I have my eyes on all of you and whoever commits an evil act against women will be punished."

Vivek stifled a laugh. "So who are you? Some kind of a vigilante or a Wonder Woman with hundred eyes who can see inside each and every household and family in Mumbai?"

"I am just a housewife, but yes, I have more than a hundred eyes," said Antara.

"Why are you doing this?"

Antara spoke in a heavy voice. "It's been five years since Nirbhaya. A lot of protests, debates and discussions have happened. But nothing seems to have changed. Crimes against women have only turned more heinous and ghastlier. Rapists prefer to kill the victim and not leave any evidence behind. The government and the entire system have failed to protect women in our society, so I am doing my bit."

Vivek was amused and asked, "So how do you do all this?"

Antara smiled, saying, "I have my unique powers, just like Wonder Woman, Superman or Spiderman."

Vivek laughed out loud this time. "And what do you call yourself?"

Antara spoke with a straight face, "Housewife."

"Hmm. You mean to say that you also killed Jimmy Mistry and Amrit Shah?"

"Yes, I killed them and even made Jimmy write the suicide note," said Antara casually.

"And they all listened to you?" asked Vivek.

"I told you, I have my powers," said Antara.

"So who are you targeting next?"

"Like I told you, it's a warning for all men who ill-treat women."

And she cut the call.

29

Pranav Dhiwar, Senior Inspector, Crime Branch, Mumbai Police, sat listening to Vivek as he told the cop about the call he had received.

The inspector heard him with a straight face and nodded thoughtfully. Finally, he said, "Sirji, I saw your 9 p.m. show. You and your panel of experts concluded that stress levels are increasing in society and there's no dearth of lunatics in the city."

"Yes, so?" asked Vivek.

The inspector smiled, "Sirji, that housewife could be one of those lunatics. I mean, which housewife would go out to target rapists, wife-beaters and cheaters?"

"Your own officer was killed," said Vivek.

"We all knew about Shinde's addiction to alcohol and young girls. It was only a matter of time. It was good that he was dismissed and took his own life," said Dhiwar.

"This housewife told me she wrote 'I AM A RAPIST' on his face," said Vivek.

The inspector bent close towards him, "We all know a beggar girl was brought in for Shinde. It was that girl who did it. I heard you were in the lock-up that night."

Vivek was quiet.

"The housewife told me that she pushed Amrit Shah and made Jimmy Mistry write the suicide note," said Vivek.

"The police and the forensics team have thoroughly examined the crime scenes in all cases," said Dhiwar. "There were no signs of anyone else being present. Tell me, how could anyone get inside Amrit Shah's house, walk into the balcony, push him down to his death, and then safely move out without being noticed by anyone. The building has security guards and cameras all over the place. In fact, we checked all the CCTV footage and there is no sign of anyone else entering or going out of the house."

Vivek looked confused. "She told me this is a warning to all men who ill-treat women. She sounded convincing, serious."

"All maniacs sound convincing," said Dhiwar. "Forget about her."

"I thought the police could at least do a check on her," said Vivek.

Dhiwar smiled. "She called you from a public phone booth, so it's difficult to trace her. The number you gave us belongs to a booth near Goregaon railway station."

"I live in Goregaon East," spoke out Vivek.

"See, it could be any of those women with an eye for you or just plain jealous of your wife because she has such a successful and caring husband," said the inspector.

Vivek shook his head in disappointment.

"She called herself a housewife, didn't give you any name...Do you know how many housewives are there in Mumbai? Most of them have problems in marriages. Anyone could have gone to Goregaon railway station and called you to vent out their frustration."

Vivek remained quiet.

"Sirji, why are you taking so much stress.

You do your work, let the police do theirs," said Dhiwar.

"Let's not make too much out of these suicide cases. It seems you have been giving too much of thought to these with your TV show and all. My advice to you, go home, take two large shots of whiskey and sleep. I assure you everything will be okay in the morning."

Vivek nodded and shook hands with Dhiwar. "I'll try to sleep."

But he walked out of the police station thinking, *"What if this housewife is real?"*

He walked ahead, taking in the late night's fresh air and silence. He saw the wine shop pulling down the shutter and rushed to it. He bought a 250 ml bottle of whiskey, and taking the inspector's advice, sipped on it before entering the house. He knew his wife wouldn't like seeing him stressed and drinking like this. He changed, went straight to the bed, and slept.

The housewife turned to look at him and smiled.

30

Dr Ankit Bhushan placed the surgical instruments in a tray and kept them close to the operating table. He switched on the spherical light above. He was one of the most well-known gynaecologists in Mumbai, with his private nursing home in Andheri West, Lokhandwala. He had reputed clientele of all TV actresses and media persons.

It was almost 3 p.m. His staff had finished their lunch and was busy gossiping or checking messages on WhatsApp. He was preparing for the most important surgery of his lifetime.

He locked the OT from inside and looked at the operating table. Everything seemed ready for the surgery.

Ankit Bhushan walked to the table and lay down on it. This time it was his turn. He picked up a scalpel and looked at it with shiny eyes. He raised his hand slowly and slit one wrist and then the other. Soon, blood started to gush out of his veins and drip down across the floor. Bhushan closed his eyes.

Across the city, Vivek was working in his office, preparing a line-up for the next news bulletin when his cell phone buzzed. "Hello."

"You thought I am a lunatic housewife? A mental case telling you suicide stories?" he heard the deep-throated voice, a chill running down his spine. "I told you I'm going to punish all rapists, wife-beaters and cheaters."

"I'm not interested in your stupid stories," shouted Vivek.

"If you are not interested, I won't waste your time. But I thought you would be interested to know that Dr Ankit Bhushan, who owns Mother's Pride Clinic in Lokhandwala, has slit his wrists. Even as we speak, he is lying in his operation theatre with blood flowing out of his body. He might survive if he gets help in time, or he just might die. Would you like to help him?"

"What?" Vivek stammered. "Why?"

"Like I told you earlier, he is a cheater. And you know what cheaters deserve."

With that, the phone call was cut.

A eunuch walked out from the phonebooth near Andheri railway station. He had the same strange glazed eyes. He walked into the huge crowd walking towards the railway station.

"Housewife," mumbled Vivek. "Damn!" he shouted and called up Pranav Dhiwar to go check on Mother's Pride.

Vivek searched for the contact details of the clinic on the Internet and called to tell them to check their operation theatre.

The girl at the reception thought it was a crank call, but still called out to a cleaning boy and asked him to check on Dr Bhushan in the OT. The cleaner boy checked the door and found it locked from inside.

"Doctor sa'ab is busy inside. There must be some surgery going on," he reported.

The receptionist looked at the schedule, "But there's no surgery scheduled at this time." She called out to a nurse and asked her to go and check.

"There must be some personal guest," the nurse said with a smile. They all knew what that meant.

The receptionist went back to work.

It took twenty-minutes for the first police van to reach the clinic. Dhiwar knew it would be difficult for him to reach there in time, so he called the nearest police post and asked them to run and check.

The police team rushed towards the OT. The door was locked from inside. The hawaldaar told his constables to break open the door. After a few attempts, the door gave way.

There was a pool of blood on the floor. The body seemed ashen, totally drained of blood. The nurses and other doctors rushed to check on the police and cried out at seeing Bhushan lying on the operating table with his wrists slit. They wanted to rush in and help but the police stopped them.

"This is a crime scene. We can't allow you to enter," said the hawaldaar.

"He needs help or he might die," cried a nurse.

By this time Dhiwar had also reached the

clinic and saw the ghastly scene. He allowed one of the assistant doctors to walk in with him, making sure not to step on blood. The junior doctor checked on Bhushan's pulse and shook his head. "He's dead."

Vivek was rushing towards the clinic. He called up inspector and asked hopefully, "Have you reached?"

"Yes, but we were late. He's dead."

31

The police found the scalpel with which Bhushan slit his wrists. The fingerprints on the scalpel matched the doctor's. Forensics picked up prints from other instruments, the light switches, the bottles, even hair from the operating table. Everything matched with Bhushan.

Prima facie, it was a clear case of death by suicide.

'But the housewife called me and said it was she who killed the doctor," said Vivek.

Dhiwar was puzzled. "How is it even possible? The door was locked from inside. There are no windows or any other doors in the operation theatre that she could have slipped out from."

"I have no clue," said Vivek.

"Could it be that she hypnotizes her victims into killing themselves? I read it in a novel. And a trigger word made the victim do what he was asked, as if in a trance," the inspector said excitedly.

Vivek looked at him amazed. "This is not a detective novel. You think a housewife can just walk in and hypnotize the victims and then walk out without being noticed? Even on CCTV cameras you have not been able to find any person, man or woman close to their victims before they killed themselves."

"Except for Leena," said the inspector.

"She was not present here. That clears her from this case," said Vivek. "I have checked the number she called me from this time. It's a phonebooth near Andheri railway station. We can check all the phonebooths and ask them to give us the description of the woman who made a call at this time."

"I'll send my men there," said inspector.

"I hope we catch her," said Vivek. "The housewife killed this doctor to make us realize that she is serious and not a lunatic."

"How did she know that we think she is a lunatic?" asked the inspector.

Vivek was stunned. "She told me that. But how did she know?"

"This is crazy," said Dhiwar.

A hawaldaar walked in with a cell phone packed in a plastic pouch, saying, "Sirji, this is the doctor's cell. We found a whole lot of pictures on this and one recording."

The inspector carefully took out the phone and switched it on. He browsed through the image gallery and saw nude images of many young girls and women. He looked at the voice recordings. There was only one.

"I'm Dr Ankit Bhushan," the dead man's voice filled the room. "I'm a gynaecologist, who is trusted by most women and mothers. I have made a fortune treating them. However, I broke their trust by taking their nude pictures and even started blackmailing them to have sex with me. I would bring them to the operation theatre in my clinic and force them to strip and lie down on the table. I not only violated these girls and women but also cheated on my wife and broke her trust. I am ashamed of myself and realize that I don't deserve to live. So, right here inside the OT, on the same operating table, I'm ending my life. I'm slitting my wrists with the scalpel. I hope you all can forgive me."

"Another suicide note," said Vivek.

"How does she manage to make them write or record without anyone noticing her," said the inspector.

"Sir, I think she makes them have some kind of drug under whose influence they do as they are told," said the hawaldaar. "I read it on WhatsApp. Nowadays, new drugs keep coming. Even sportsmen take drugs."

The inspector gave him a look. The hawaldaar shrugged and walked away.

"Let's hope we get a description from the phonebooth," said the inspector. "Do keep me informed if she calls you again."

"Sure," said Vivek, getting up. He shook hands with the inspector and walked out.

As Vivek was driving back to his office, his phone rang. "Yes," said Vivek.

"I'm sure you do not have any more doubts about me. I'm not a lunatic. I'm a housewife," said the heavy voice. "I have more than a hundred eyes and ears."

32

The three police constables of Inspector Dhiwar's team sat in a semi-circle as their boss sipped on his extra-sweet cutting chai. They were all silent, munching on vada pav and sipping hot tea.

"I am hundred per cent sure it is drugs," said Hawaldaar Ram Kumar Peth. "Amrit Shah and Jimmy Mistry both used to take drugs; and Inspector Shinde was a drunkard who also used drugs. Sirji, my theory is right. This woman is using drugs to make them do things. Nowadays there are so many types of drugs – rape drug, date drug, sex drug; this could be a new one."

The constables nodded in agreement and waited for their sa'ab to say something.

"*Saala chutiya*, how would she even give the drug to all those *gandus* to kill themselves? She was not seen anywhere near them," said the inspector.

"Sir," one of the constables raised his hand, "It could be a ghost. There are those *ichchadhari naagin* types who come back to take revenge. It seems this housewife was killed by her husband and her spirit has come to take revenge on all these evil men."

Dhiwar looked at him. "Do you beat your wife? Have you raised your hand at her?"

The constable fumbled. "At times, when she does too much bickering, then I give her one."

"It is your number next," the inspector smiled. The others laughed.

"There's nothing to laugh about. I know where you all go after your duty, to that red-light area. She is also targeting cheats," said Dhiwar.

The constables looked at each other, a bit scared. One of them spoke out, "Sir, did this housewife ever call you?"

"No."

"I knew it. There's no housewife. There's

no killer targeting rapists, wife-beaters, and cheaters," said the constable.

"What do you mean?"

"Sirji, you were told this 'housewife' story by that reporter. I am sure he made it up. In fact, he is after these suicides which could be murders," said the constable.

"How can you say that?" asked the inspector.

"I saw a film where a reporter started targeting and killing prominent figures. Obviously, only he had the news about the murders, so he used to print it in his newspaper and soon his newspaper circulation skyrocketed. He has also been doing exclusive coverage of all these cases and the ratings of his channel have gone up. Right now, they are number one, sir."

The others seemed to agree, saying, "He's correct. These news channel *walas* can do anything for ratings. He has to be involved in all this. There's no housewife."

Antara, who was sitting on a table near them in her spirit form, smiled before taking her place in side a constable who suddenly walked up to the inspector. "You can't even solve one case. You are an idiot," he shouted.

Dhiwar was furious at how his constable was casting doubts on his abilities. He jumped on the constable, pushing him down. Even as the other men looked at the pair in shock.

Antara then moved into the hawaldaar, making him pick up his stick and beat the three constables. "How dare you attack my sa'ab? I'm going to kill you all," he shouted.

The inspector, totally puzzled by the uncharacteristic behaviour of his men, yelled, "Stop it! Stop it, you idiots."

To this the hawaldaar turned to him with his stick and was about to hit him when Antara moved out of him. The man collapsed on the floor, as if dead.

The policemen looked at each other confused.

The constable mumbled, "I'm telling you, sir, it seems our chai was drugged. The housewife keeping a watch on us."

33

Leena was sweating as she ran on the treadmill dressed in tights and a short top, revealing her thin waist and sculpted arms.

Vivek ran around the machines, as the guards chased him.

Leena was shocked seeing him there. She stopped the treadmill and turned to look at him. "What do you want now? You got your interview."

Vivek shouted, "Leena, I'm sorry that I suspected you. I have found the killer, who murdered the men and turned them into suicides. Your husband was also killed. He was murdered."

Leena raised her hand to stop the guards and told them to back off. "Okay, let's hear what you have to say."

The guards backed off and stood at a distance, watching him.

Vivek walked cautiously towards Leena and said, "There's a housewife targeting rapists, wife-beaters, cheats, and all men who ill-treat women. She punishes them as per their evil acts. In some cases, she has killed them and made it look like suicide. She called me. When I refused to take her seriously, she killed a doctor in Andheri and again made it look like a suicide."

"Don't give me your bullshit. I don't have time for your crap. Leave," said Leena, turning away.

The guards moved to hold him, but Vivek ran behind the rack of heavy weights, "Leena, trust me. I'm telling you the truth. Even your husband was killed by her. I only want a few minutes to explain it all."

Leena stopped and looked at him, "You are losing your mind. You shouldn't be in the media business. I have already told the police; I was there with my husband in the balcony. Please don't keep reminding me of what happened that day."

"You said in your statement that you were unconscious, that Shah jumped off the balcony to his death," said Vivek. "You obviously didn't see anyone as you were unconscious. It could be that someone sneaked into your house and was hiding somewhere? The person waited for the right time and pushed him over and disappeared?"

"The police checked all the CCTV placed in the lobby, the corridors and all around the building. They didn't find anyone who could have gone up to the fiftieth floor," said Leena.

"Well, this is the mystery I'm trying to solve. How does this housewife get in without being seen or even caught by the cameras all over the place? That too in this day and age. I'm sure that the killer is still out there and more men will be killed. We won't be able to do anything."

"And this killer is a woman who calls herself Housewife?" asked Leena.

"Yes, she has called me a few times. She considers herself to be some sort of vigilante, ridding the society of evil men."

"Being a woman, I'm proud of her," said Leena. "Isn't she doing a great service to society? The only thing is to accomplish her mission she might have to kill the entire male population."

"You believe every man is a rapist, beater or a cheater?" asked Vivek.

"All men have that streak in them. It surfaces at times," said Leena. "Well, leave that aside. What do you want from me?"

"I came here to tell you that your husband might have been murdered and that there's a murderer roaming the streets, killing men. We have to stop this Housewife. The police are conducting their own investigation, but we can investigate too. I need your help."

Leena laughed out loud. "So now you want us to turn into a Sherlock and Watson? Will that help your channel garner more ratings? I'm sure with the CEO of Lotus Enterprises in tow it would turn out to be a hell of a story."

"My only aim is to catch this killer. The very fact that she was not noticed entering or exiting your house could mean that she was known to your husband," said Vivek. He looked at her and hesitatingly added, "What if they were having an affair? This Housewife claims to have killed Jimmy Mistry too and that she forced him to write his suicide note."

Leena sat down on one of the benches, taking a long breath. "Okay, Sherlock, tell me what I have to do?"

Vivek excitedly bent down on his knees, "See, we don't have any evidence or clues. I want to look through all of Shah's stuff, whatever is there, big or small. Maybe we'll find something there. We need one little ray of hope. I'm sure we will make it through."

"That sounds interesting. Let me see what I can do," said Leena.

"It's time to act not think, or this Housewife will kill more men," said Vivek.

Leena looked at him, "That would lessen a whole lot of burden from this planet. I like this Housewife. Even I was a housewife once."

34

Antara had planned to treat Vivek with his favourite hot pooris with *chholey* and *boondi raita*. After all, he was working day and night, trailing the Housewife. She had brought gulab jamuns from the most expensive sweet shop. She wanted to indulge in pillow talk with him and then sleep in his arms. She had regained her confidence since she had donned the mantle of the Housewife. She was feeling productive.

Antara had started to meet with other women and would play with their kids. Even their comments didn't bother her anymore. Soon the women stopped commenting. They found her to be happy and cheerful. Antara had turned into a totally carefree woman who never complained about her husband or in-laws. She was a woman on a mission. She realised the hollowness of the many women who survived on gossip and felt pity for them.

Antara was the CEO of her life. It started with one of the wives in the building coming to her for advice. It opened the flood gates. Soon other women poured in, seeking advice to sort out their troubled marriages, relationship with kids and in-laws. She turned into somewhat of an agony aunt. She enjoyed the role and was actually good at it. Her reality was of a housewife.

Vivek walked in late at night and Antara served him hot dinner. He didn't seem interested but couldn't resist the smell. By the time Antara brought out the hot gulab jaamuns, Vivek was beaming and talking animatedly about his work and boss. It was Antara's mother who had advised her to feed the husband his favourite dishes so he would never go astray. Somehow all women turn out to be like their mothers and all men like their fathers.

They sat at the table talking for almost two hours. Vivek burped and farted. Antara laughed. It was a sign that he was content and happy. But Vivek was on guard throughout their conversation. He didn't mention the Housewife, Leena or even that he planned to investigate the Housewife.

After all, Antara was a model housewife. She didn't bicker, nag or even try to make him talk. She knew everything. She was the Housewife.

As they were retiring to the bedroom, Vivek's cell phone rang. It was Inspector Dhiwar. "The police team got a description of the person who made the call from the phonebooth outside Andheri railway station. A eunuch. The phonebooth operator said that the eunuch was a regular and made a call at exactly the same time every day. Eunuchs beg for money in local trains and they had to keep their boss updated."

Vivek was confused. "She had a heavy voice, but a eunuch?"

"We rounded up the eunuch, but she has no idea about any housewife. In fact, she laughed at us for calling her a housewife. We also checked with other vendors at Andheri station and they all know her pretty well. She travels in local trains from morning to evening collecting alms. There seems to be a mistake, Vivek, and the police cannot waste any more time investigating this Housewife," said the inspector.

"But she is hell bent on killing more men," said Vivek.

"What I know is whatever you have told me. Maybe you are making up these stories to spice up your news show. We have no evidence to suggest that any other person is involved in all these cases. They are all suicides. If you persist with such false stories, I will have to take action against you," Dhiwar warned.

Vivek fought for words to convince the inspector, but the man cut the call.

Antara could sense his frustration. She had wanted to give him the biggest story of his life—the housewife. But he could not put it on air without evidence. In that he was on his own. A housewife can be supportive, loving and caring, but she won't spoon-feed you all the time.

Of course, that didn't stop her from preparing his lunch box the next morning. She even packed an apple and a bottle of buttermilk.

Vivek looked at the tiffin and laughed, "What the hell is this? You know I order lunch from outside. Don't bother cooking and preparing all this early in the morning."

"I like to do it. Also, I don't want you to eat food from outside. After all, nothing is better than homecooked food," said Antara.

Vivek knew there was no use telling her. He picked up his bag and the heavy lunch bag. Just as he was about to leave, the doorbell rang and Vivek opened it to see a middle-aged obese lady standing there with two heavy bags filled with varied savouries.

"I have the best of khaakra, paapad, farsaan and pickle. Everything is home made," she said.

Vivek turned to look at Antara. "See, even aunty has all homemade stuff."

The next second the woman had barged in and taken out a long knife. She pointed the knife at Vivek, "*Ae chokri,* get me all your jewellery and cash or I'm going to cut his throat."

The woman waved her knife menacingly near Vivek's throat.

Vivek was scared and nervous. He tried to speak up, but the woman cut him short, "Don't try to act smart, this knife is smarter.

It'll cut you up pretty fast." She looked at Antara and shouted, "Why are you still standing here? Get me all your jewellery and cash."

Antara rushed inside the room and opened her cupboard. She threw down her clothes looking for her jewellery box and some cash.

Vivek spoke softly, keeping his eyes on the woman, "Madamji, this is not right. I'm a reporter with a news channel and I'll report it to the police. You won't be able to run and hide."

The woman looked at him and got angry, "You want me to turn out your intestines? Or should I cut your face so bad that you will never be able to report on TV? Let me do my work and I'll..."

Suddenly, the woman's eyes lit up. She lowered the hand holding the knife and dropped it. With that she started spinning on the spot with increasing speed. In that same motion she opened the door and rushed out and onto the stairs, falling head down. She went tumbling to the ground floor.

Vivek called up the guards on the intercom, telling them to catch hold of the woman coming down the stairs. "She's a thief."

The guards ran and held the woman. The police were called and Vivek gave his statement, handing them the knife with which she had threatened them. But he couldn't explain the sudden change in her behaviour and her spinning and rushing out of the house.

"It's all due to Mata's blessings. Last week Mummy had gone to Vaishno Mata and see how Mata protected us." Antara dismissed his concern and cried out loud, *"Jai Mata di."*

The burglar lady herself was puzzled and stunned by what had happened. Her modus operandi had never failed her.

"Now I can tell that Housewife that it's not always the men who are bad. Some women too are evil," Vivek mumbled.

"Yes, there are lot of women who are criminals, but men are getting sicker by the day."

Vivek looked at her and nodded. "Hail woman kind! I better leave now. I have a lot of work to do."

35

The beauties stood in a line, all covered. There were seven of them, including a Mercedes, BMW, Porsche, Land Rover and Hummer.

Leena had called Vivek over to start their investigation by going through them. These were owned by Amrit Shah, and they had been lying in a garage gathering dust ever since his death. Leena had thought of selling them off but had never found the time or inclination to do it.

Vivek removed the covers and stared at the luxury cars. He couldn't afford one of them in fifty years. Leena handed him the keys and he opened them one by one.

"Let's start with the BMW. I'll take the driver's seat and you get in from the other side. We'll look for anything that's out of place," said Vivek.

Leena nodded.

They looked through the papers, the many compartments, inside the pouches, under the seats, under the mats, inside the boot and bonnet. They searched each car thoroughly but couldn't find anything that might connect a woman with Amrit Shah.

By the end they were too tired to look anywhere else. Vivek told her that he needed to look at the fiftieth-floor apartment where she stayed with Amrit.

"The police have already gone through it with a fine-toothed comb," said Leena.

"They were not looking for what we are looking for," said Vivek. "Please. It might be useful and might guide us to that Housewife."

"I still can't believe he was pushed down by someone or that the person entered the house, killed him and quietly walked out," said Leena.

"You were unconscious. Maybe you were drugged," said Vivek.

Leena countered, "I was unconscious because Amrit had beaten me black and blue. Have you ever got beaten like that by another man?"

"I'm sorry. I didn't mean to hurt you. I am trying to question everything in the hope that it might lead us to this Housewife. What if she is using a drug?"

"Or what if she hypnotizes people into dying by suicide like it happens in crime shows on television," said Leena.

Vivek was reminded of the police constable saying the very same things.

"Okay, forget it," said Vivek. "We can still look at the apartment."

"That would be the last of this investigation, Sherlock. If you don't find anything there, this is over. I won't allow you anywhere near my properties again. Are we clear?" she said sternly.

"Yes, we are clear."

The Housewife sat in her spirit form in a corner, watching them. She was amused, and smiled. She loved to see Vivek posing as a detective. Leena might tease him with it, but for her, he was Sherlock.

36

The fiftieth-floor apartment had been locked since Amrit Shah's death. The police, after their investigation, had cleared the crime scene and had given full authorisation to Leena to use the apartment. However, Leena had opted to move out.

It was a 3,300 square feet house with five bedrooms and a study. Not many people owned this big a house in Mumbai. All five bedrooms had sea-facing large windows with a balcony. There were paintings on the wall, artefacts and antiques on display, huge vases from China and Mongolia, a glass case filled with crystals from all over the world, one wall was covered with hand-painted masks and the tiles on the floor shined like mirrors. All in all, it was an expensive house.

Leena showed him the rooms, kitchen, study, and the large living room. The study was where Amrit spent a lot of time doing his paperwork and making calls and, at times, reading books. It was the perfect place to start.

They started going through the drawers of the study table. Vivek looked at files and papers and Leena checked the books and the bookcase. They moved to look behind the paintings on the wall and into the chest of drawers placed in the room. Nothing.

Vivek moved to the couple's bedroom and checked the wardrobes. It still had a lot of clothes and dresses. He looked behind the clothes and under the stack of towels. He checked the shoe rack. Nothing.

They checked the other rooms. They ransacked the whole place, but they didn't find anything to connect Amrit to a woman or lead them to the Housewife.

Finally, they were back in the living room.

Leena looked at him and said, "I hope you are satisfied now. There's nothing here. Now we can go our own ways and forget all this. I hope you know each of my days is worth a few millions. Every hour I lose, I lose millions."

Vivek nodded quietly. He sat there thoughtfully for a moment and suddenly got up. "I want to check one last thing."

He walked to the wardrobe inside the master bedroom and opened it to bring out a wallet. He had seen the wallet but hadn't checked it. Even the police hadn't bothered to check it. It was a case of suicide. He showed it to Leena and she confirmed it belonged to Amrit.

Vivek removed its contents carefully. There were a few pictures of gods, a stack of credit and debit cards, a few two-thousand-and-five-hundred-rupee notes, a few slips of credit card transactions and finally a small key. A single key.

Vivek showed it to Leena. "Have you seen this before?"

"No."

"Good," said Vivek. "Let's try and see if it fits somewhere in the house."

He went around trying the key in each and every lock he could find inside the house. The key didn't fit into any of them.

Vivek looked at the key closely and saw some initials on the key that had faded. He used his phone camera to zoom into the initials. "Something Homes."

"It belongs to a house or a flat. The first word is not clear but the second is clearly homes," said an excited Vivek.

"So what does that mean?" asked Leena.

"Amrit kept a single key to a house in his wallet that even you didn't know about. Why would anyone keep a single key in his wallet? It has to be something very personal. We have to find this place. Maybe more connections and clarity will emerge from there. So tell me, what other properties did he own in Mumbai?"

"I have no idea of any other flats or apartments in Mumbai. He didn't believe in investing money in properties. He made all his money from the share market and he understood trading better than property," said Leena. "He used to have three flats, but he had to sell them off when he suffered losses."

"But he still carried this single key in his wallet. It can't be for sentimental value," said Vivek.

"He was not at all sentimental. He was a hardcore businessman. If this key was there in his wallet, it means it was important to him," said Leena.

"It has to be a bank locker," shouted Vivek.

"All bank lockers were in my name. Don't forget the initials on the key."

Vivek moved around thoughtfully. Suddenly he turned to Leena, "Did he drive or did he have a driver?"

"Amrit had a driver who worked with him for the last ten years," said Leena.

"The driver has to know. After all, he took Amrit to all the places in Mumbai or nearby cities and towns," said Vivek. "You'll have to call this driver."

37

The driver pointed towards a building in Santa Cruz East, "Madam, this is the building Amrit sa'ab used to come to. He had warned me never to mention it to you."

"What's the flat number," asked Vivek.

"I don't know, sa'ab. I never went inside with him. He would always ask me to wait outside," said the driver.

"Let's go in," Vivek said.

They walked inside the lobby and asked for Amrit Shah's flat. "I heard on the news that Amrit sa'ab is no more," the guard said.

"Yes, and this is his wife. She wants to check the flat," said Vivek curtly.

The guard softened, "It's 1104 on the eleventh floor." They got into the lift and went up to eleventh floor. Leena walked towards the flat and stopped near the main door. "I had no idea he owned this flat."

Leena hesitatingly put the key in the lock. It went in smoothly and seemed like a perfect fit. She rotated it and pushed open the door. They walked inside to see a furnished flat with furniture, white goods and other gadgets. Inside the bedroom was a large double bed with a sixteen-inch-thick mattress. The kitchen was fully equipped too.

"What was he doing here? Why didn't he tell me about it?" Leena wondered aloud.

Vivek started to inspect the wardrobes and drawers, trying to look for something to hold on to. The wardrobes were filled with skimpy female dresses, a few school uniforms for girls, and stacks of undergarments. Vivek looked through the cabinets and finally found a small diary. There were many phone numbers scrawled on its pages with each number was given a code name – X, XX, XXX, X1, X2 and others.

Vivek was puzzled. He dialled one number and hurriedly cut the call. He turned to look at Leena. "Your husband used to bring in call girls here. This seems to be his little harem. All these numbers belong to those girls."

Leena had tears in her eyes. "What happened to him? Why would he do this? I knew he was a drunkard and a drug addict. He even abused me and beat me, but I never thought he would be doing this secretly."

Vivek consoled her. "This is the reason why that Housewife targeted him. We have to find her. It could be one of those escorts seeking revenge. There has to be something else here."

Vivek started to look in other places. Leena was heartbroken. Her tears kept flowing. Manpreet called her to inquire about where she was, but Leena cut her call.

In another cabinet, Vivek found pictures of nude young girls with Amrit Shah. He came out and showed them to Leena saying, "Look, these are the girls. He kept these pictures hidden in a cabinet. Now we will be able to trace and question them."

Leena was totally broken. Her sobs didn't seem to stop. She started to speak incoherently, "Throughout our marriage, I kept giving him all the leeway. I thought he would change and would stop abusing me and give up his drug addiction. Nothing changed. I was all alone in that marriage. Even after his death, I had to fight to take over the business. The entire board of directors were against me. Even today they are looking for opportunities to throw me out. Every day has become a fight for me to survive in this man's world. At times I think that I should give it all up and go away. Manpreet is the only source of strength I have in my life. She keeps telling me to keep moving and fight them. Now this. I don't know whether I'll ever be able to pick up the broken pieces. I always wanted a family. And here I am with nothing. Nobody to love and care for. Nobody loves me."

Vivek rushed to her and hugged her tight. "I understand you. I'm there with you in this. I won't ever leave you."

Leena looked at him with teary eyes and hugged him tight. They stood holding each other for some time. Leena looked at him and said, "It seems like ages since I hugged a man. I even forgot the touch of a man. Maybe I have also forgotten to love and be loved. I have become this marble statue that looks perfect, sculpted from the outside but broken and misshapen inside."

Vivek wiped her tears with his hands. "You are so beautiful, Leena. Anyone would love you or go mad for you. You are a beautiful person."

"You really think so or are saying it for effect?"

"I mean it," said Vivek.

"See, I'm used to so much flattery that I have forgotten what's genuine and what not."

Vivek looked into her eyes and kissed her on the lips. "This is genuine."

Leena kept looking at him and he kissed her again.

38

Sanjay Singh, a property dealer with his office at the newly developed Kandivali East, walked into his small flat. He had brought a stack of papers home. He called out to his wife, Suneeta. They had migrated from Lucknow to Mumbai fifteen years ago. Suneeta had grown obese but was a loving wife and had given him three kids.

Suneeta brought out a glass of water on a tray as any good housewife does the moment their husband enters the house. "Would you like some tea or nimbu pani?" she asked.

Sanjay told her to sit. He had something important to talk to her about. Suneeta sat close to him and started speaking, "I hope you remember we have to deposit the school fees and Pooja is going on her first school trip to Panchgani. They need five thousand rupees for the trip."

"Don't worry. I'll take care of that," said Sanjay.

Sanjay pushed the pile of papers in front of her, "You have to sign these."

"What are these?" asked Suneeta.

Sanjay looked at her. "Divorce papers."

Suneeta was shocked. Her face changed. She had tears in her eyes.

"See, it's been more than eighteen years that we have been married. Look at yourself, you can hardly walk properly. We haven't had any sex in the last three years. I can't live with you like this. I need love in my life. I need this divorce, and there are other papers where you give me full ownership rights over this house," said Sanjay.

She started crying, tears flowed out of her eyes. "Where will I go? We have three kids. My family will be devastated. Don't do this, please."

Sanjay remained expressionless. "You had better stop with this drama of yours. I have had enough of you. I cannot go on like this. I need a better life. It would be better for us that we do this mutually and go our separate ways."

Suneeta kept looking at him and then her eyes flashed. Her tone changed. "You want a divorce and ownership of this house? This house belongs to me and my kids. I gave you eighteen years of my life and suddenly you seem to have found some young girl and want to get rid of me? I'm not going to sign these papers and I'll not divorce you."

Antara had found out Sanjay Singh's secret life. He had found a forty-year-old divorcee. They had planned to divorce his wife and sell off his old flat in Meera Road to start their new life in an upcoming locality. Sanjay had started showering her with gifts and forgotten to deposit their kids' school fees.

Antara thought he would change for his children if not the wife, but nothing seemed to change. He was there with divorce papers and to take over the house.

Sanjay laughed at his wife saying, "What will you do? I'm going to file for divorce in court. You want to drag the kids to court. Is that what you want? This is the easiest solution that we can agree upon inside the walls of the house. Nobody will even get to know. You can go back to your parents' house in Bareilly."

Suneeta started crying, "I will never leave my house and kids. I will not let you divorce me."

Sanjay got irritated and shouted at her, "Don't raise your voice. It was me who deigned to marry you. No other man would even come near a fat woman like you."

"Yes, you married me because my father gave you ten lakh rupees with which you shifted to Mumbai and started your office here."

"Don't give me your *paisa-ka-dhauns* or I'm going to hit you," said Sanjay angrily.

Suneeta picked up her son's cricket bat and raised it at Sanjay, "*Saale*, try and touch me and I'll break your head."

"You are going to hit me?" cried an enraged Sanjay. He pounced at her and Suneeta whacked the bat at him. The bat caught him in the ribs and he went down.

Suneeta's eyes were shining bright. She looked furious. "Get up and show me your manliness now, you bastard. You've always hit me whenever you wanted. Now try and touch me."

Sanjay got up and tried to grab the bat but Suneeta hit him on the legs. Sanjay cried out and rushed out to the stairs, "I'm going to file a police complaint against you."

As he rushed down Suneeta chased after him. She caught up with him right in the middle of the building complex. She started to beat him with the bat.

The kids returning from school rushed to her crying, "Maa, what are you doing?"

She kept hitting Sanjay and said, "Your father wants to divorce me for some other woman and wants to take away our house to give it to that bitch. I'll not let it happen."

Other people from the housing society crowded around. Suneeta warned Sanjay in front of the crowd, "Don't you dare take my kids away from me or their house. I'll break each and every bone in your body. Now get lost and don't ever come here. I'll take care of my family without you."

Suneeta walked inside the building with her kids. Her children had never seen her like this. They had always seen her as a submissive woman who gave in to every whim of their father. They had not seen the spirit that had taken possession of their mother.

It was the Housewife, empowering other housewives.

39

The video of Suneeta beating her husband with a cricket bat had gone viral. It was recorded by one of the women in the building. She had uploaded it on her WhatsApp groups and it had spread all across the city. With the video, messages of women groups against men seeking divorce to marry younger girls started pouring in. The housewives were getting closely knit, forming committees to fight against domestic violence and other atrocities.

A channel had even interviewed Suneeta, who, although shell-shocked, had found strength in the women reaching out to her. "I have been reminded that I should not put myself or my children through such abuse.

My mother used to tell me this. I am certain it was my mother who showed me the courage at that moment when my life flashed in front of my eyes as my husband beat me," she said. "I will find a way to move on, but no longer suffer that man's insults."

It was late in the night. Vivek and Antara sat at the dining table watching the video on Vivek's phone.

Antara kept laughing. "These men need to be beaten like this. How can they even think of divorcing wives who have stood by them for over eighteen years? It's good the housewives are getting together and empowering themselves. They need to be economically independent too. Then these men won't be able to pin them down."

"Suddenly, this housewife has become aware of her rights and is getting more powerful," said Vivek. "You know there's one housewife who is targeting all men who are rapists, wife-beaters, and cheaters. She has killed a few and made it all look like suicides."

"I don't believe it. A housewife cannot do it," said Antara.

"Well, even I don't believe it. But just to prove her point she killed a doctor and called me to confirm," said Vivek.

"What about the police?"

"The police think I'm making up this story. They couldn't find any evidence against anyone in all the cases. In fact, there's no sign of any break-in where these men were killed. I'm puzzled. How did she do it?"

"Well, the point is not what she is doing but whether it is right or not," said Antara.

"What is right about killing people?"

"You said she is targeting evil men. They must be really vile that she went as far as killing them," said Antara.

"I know they were all evil in their own way, but this housewife can't take the law in her hands. She can't dispense justice. There are courts and police for this," said Vivek.

"The police won't even believe you, a senior editor of a reputed news channel. You think they would ever believe a housewife? Sometimes one has to fight."

"Fighting does not mean killing," said Vivek.

"Every day we throw out garbage from our homes. Even the society needs to be rid of these men who are no less than garbage. I am with this housewife," said Antara.

Vivek looked at her and smiled, "I have never seen you and heard you speaking so spiritedly. This housewife is surely having a big impact on housewives in the city. It seems even this Suneeta was inspired by her in some way to beat up her husband."

Antara nodded. "Finally, women will have to take charge. It's more important for a housewife. After all, she is dependent on her husband to provide for her while she toils all day in the house."

"Okay, so tell me...Are you not happy with me? Do I trouble you? Give you too much stress? I know most of the times I am caught up chasing news stories and you might feel a bit lonely. However, I hope I have not given you any reason to complain," asked Vivek, a little hesitant.

"Oh, come on, Vivek. I love you and I love cooking for you and keeping the house beautiful so you can relax, be happy, and we have a good time when you are home. I know your work is very important for you."

Vivek smiled, looking at her. "What if I fall in love with some young, beautiful girl and want to divorce you?"

"I'll call the Housewife," said Antara.

40

Early next morning, Manpreet sat with Leena sipping coffee, "What has happened to you? You missed two big meetings with investors. Everyone has been asking about you and I have had to make up stories that you were not well."

Leena signed a few documents and cheques and said, "Don't worry. Everything is under control. We haven't lost any major deal."

"So are you waiting for us to lose a big deal?" questioned Manpreet, irritated.

"There are other things in life that are also important and need to be sorted out," said Leena.

Leena's cell phone buzzed and she saw it was Vivek calling. Manpreet too saw his name flash on the cell phone, "Now you have his number saved?"

Leena picked up the call with a big smile on her face, "Hi, good morning. Hope you slept well. Yes, it got a bit tiring. I am working from home."

"You have been hanging out with this stupid reporter. Are you crazy? He is trying to con you into getting a story, Leena," said Manpreet.

Leena shushed her. Manpreet made a face and got up, irritated.

"I've found out that Amrit Shah visited Mahabaleshwar almost every month. There has to be some connection there," Vivek said.

"We have a bungalow there with three acres of strawberry farms. We used to go there once in a while. Amrit never told me that he visited the place every month," said Leena.

"I want us to go there and look around. We might find something. I'll wait for you at 10 near the Bandra Kurla Complex. You can pick me up," said Vivek and cut the call.

Leena turned to look at Manpreet.

Leena smiled, "Mannu, you are my closest friend. Come on, don't make such a face. I'm trying to unravel the mystery of Amrit's death. We have found some clues and are following them."

"You are playing detective-detective with that reporter," said Manpreet. "Who knows, he might be making a film and will show it on his news channel?"

"Mannu, learn to have some faith. I'm dedicated to my work and he too is to his. We have found something that might prove that Amrit was murdered by someone."

"God, Leena, you know he died by suicide," said Manpreet.

"I was unconscious at that time. I never saw him jump. Vivek's theory is that someone pushed him," said Leena.

"Okay, someone killed him and walked out without being noticed. The police did their investigation. Why are you getting embroiled in this again? It might be detrimental for the business, and what if the police want to question you again?"

"That's why we need solid evidence; to

prove I am innocent," said Leena. "I am going to Mahabaleshwar in an hour's time."

"We have an appointment with the Chief Minister today," said Manpreet. "We need his approval for our social initiative."

"You can handle that very well. I have to go to Mahabaleshwar. Get my things ready. Remember, this is between us. Don't tell anyone. It's our secret."

41

Vivek told Antara that he'd be travelling to Solapur, Satara and Kolhapur for a story on the plight of sugarcane farmers in the state. Antara was happy that Vivek was getting to do what he loved the most. They had a heavy breakfast and Vivek left with a light bag putting in one change of clothes and his toothbrush and paste.

Now free, Antara decided to see the city during its morning rush hour. In her spirit form, she saw girls and women all dressed for their schools, colleges and offices. Many of the working women travelled by local trains and had become quite adept at pushing themselves inside an already-packed compartment. The young ones even hung at the door.

Many female corporate executives drove their cars to offices in Bandra and South Mumbai. Antara was overwhelmed seeing these women taking charge of their lives. They looked confident and dressed smart, many of them even earned more than their husbands, had taken house loans and were paying EMIs, driving luxury cars and went to expensive salons and spas for their beauty treatments.

There were many policewomen on the roads, controlling traffic. She saw one female traffic constable handing a challan to a driver. Most of them were no-nonsense women. They didn't take bribes, were more punctual than men, worked more sincerely, wasted lesser time in offices, were more organised and finished their work within deadlines.

Most men in the corporate sector had started to feel threatened by this new emerging female workforce. They were driving metros, piloting aircrafts, creating software, and marketing the biggest of brands and heading the largest of banks. In fact, many a man had lost his job and now many were opting to be stay-at-home dads.

Along with these were women, who worked as labourers in the many multi-storey buildings being constructed, as prostitutes in the red-light areas, many who begged and sold trinkets at the traffic lights. There was a huge workforce of women who worked as maids, and housewives were dependent on them for their work.

In spite of the rise in women power, feminism and all, women were still easy prey. They were the ones who were hunted down, raped, molested, beaten, abused, and killed. They still were insecure, scared, and nervous in this society that had failed them repeatedly. And this was just in Mumbai, the largest cosmopolitan city in India. Forget what happened in other parts of the country.

As Antara saw these women, she went through varied emotions of awe, inspiration, power and fear. She knew each of these women was a target for some self-obsessed male. She agreed with Vivek that women could also be nasty, evil and criminal, but men outdid them.

It was at this moment that Vivek came rushing back to the house. He used his key to open the door and walked inside to collect his mobile phone that he had forgotten.

As he walked inside, he saw Antara lying on the floor. He rushed up to her and called out. There was no response. He checked her pulse. It was faint. Her breathing was shallow. "It could be a heart attack," thought Vivek. He called for an ambulance. Antara's body was put inside the ambulance and driven to the hospital.

Vivek called and informed Leena that he would get late due to an emergency.

At the hospital, Antara was rushed inside the ICU. The doctors conducted various tests and took her brain scan and heart readings to ascertain that the vital organs were functioning normally. They couldn't understand what was wrong with her and advised that it could be due to stress and that she should stay in the hospital for further tests.

Meanwhile, Antara's spirit returned to the house. She walked through the glass windows and through the walls inside the living room. She was shocked to discover her body missing. She looked through all the rooms. She had no idea what had happened. She wanted to call Vivek but realised she couldn't touch anything or pick up anything in this form.

She moved around the housing society trying to find some clue. Finally, she heard the security guards talking, "*Woh* Antara madam was a good person. Last Diwali she gave me five hundred rupees for my family. I hope she survives."

Antara was shocked. Various questions filled her head. "What happened to her body? Did someone come inside the house? Vivek had already left. Who else had the key? Is it the society president?"

She moved inside the flat of the society's president and heard him tell his wife, "*Arey*, Antara was lucky. Her husband Vivek forgot his cell in the house and came back to collect it. He found her lying on the floor. It seems like heart failure. Nowadays young people are dying. It's so sad."

Antara was thinking of ways to find where Vivek had taken her body and she saw Shagun aunty, the president's wife, walking out with a cup of tea. "I knew it. She was always tense about not becoming a mother. It's not in everyone's fate. Now look at me. All my sons are settled in the US but what's the use. They have not even called us once or have come here in the last many years. It's better not to have such kids."

Antara moved inside Shagun aunty. Shagunji picked up her mobile and dialled

Vivek's number saying, "Let me call up Vivek and ask where Antara is."

Vivek picked up the call, "Aunty, she is resting. She is better. I'm at Seven Star Hospital in Andheri East. She is in the ICU, but don't worry. She'll be fine. Thank you."

Antara moved out of her and the next moment she was inside the ICU of the hospital. She saw her body lying on the bed with a doctor checking the pulse. Various tubes and wires were attached to her body. She walked up to the bed and entered the body. Suddenly, she sat upright.

The doctors were taken aback. The nurse ran out to call Vivek. Antara looked around and said, "I'm fine, doctor. It was just weakness."

Vivek rushed inside and saw her sitting. He came towards her surprised, "You were unconscious. I brought you here in an ambulance."

Antara smiled. "I know you love me lots and will never let anything happen to me. Right now, I'm feeling fine. I want to go home, and you should carry on with your trip."

"Please, you might have some inner problem and we have to carry out more tests. I would advise you to stay here for two more days," the doctor said.

Antara removed the tubes, the needle in her arm and got up from the bed. "I feel fine. See, I can walk. I can talk." She looked at Vivek, "I want to go home, please."

Vivek nodded. "Okay. It's better that I take her home, doctor."

Back home, all the aunties, uncles and guards of the society came to meet her. The housewives brought cooked food and fruits and were all concerned about her health.

Antara told Vivek to go on his trip as he was working on an important story about farmers. Vivek agreed only when Shagunji assured him that she would be with Antara throughout the day and night. In fact, the whole society said they would take care of her.

Vivek felt reassured. He kissed Antara on her forehead and left.

Antara heaved a sigh of relief. Without her body, she would be nothing more than a ghost roaming around. She would have to be more careful in the future.

But she was sure of one thing, her husband loved her more than anything. What else does a housewife want?

42

The monsoon showers had turned the whole of Mahabaleshwar green. The place was covered with mist. It was a small hill station tucked far away from Mumbai. Most tourists kept away during the monsoon as it received heavy rains. So it was quiet enough to hear the rain falling on the tin roofs, horses neighing, and crickets singing through the night.

The bungalow was built on a hill overlooking the river with their strawberry farms stretched on one side. The mist rose from the river and enveloped the whole place. It looked like a house suspended among the clouds. Leena was thrilled to be there.

"This is so beautiful. I should come here more often," she said.

They sat on the bench in the veranda, sipping hot tea, looking at the white mist and the river. There was a chill in the air and she held onto his hand. "I hope time freezes right now and I stay here in this moment forever. I don't want to return to Mumbai to all the work and pressures."

"Don't forget you are the CEO. The businesswoman of the year," said Vivek with a smile.

"I'm also a woman. Sometimes all a woman needs is love, care, warmth, a family and a house. That's where her happiness lies. I don't have any of those. I can buy a lot of houses, but I will never have a home of my own."

"Most women in the country would love to be in your shoes."

"They don't know what they have. Family is the most precious thing they can ever have. Well, money is important, but after a point it's just numbers. At times it feels like I am only playing with numbers. They keep riding up and down. It's just a game. Not a family. Maybe that's why the Housewife targets these evil men. She understands the importance of a family and can't stand these men breaking the most sacred thing," said Leena.

They sat there for a while, staring into mist and soaking in the fresh air and rain.

Vivek thought of Antara. They were together for the last eleven years but couldn't have a family. He was caring and thoughtful, but somewhere along the way he had stopped loving her. He had taken her to the hospital and made sure she was well taken care of back in the house. That was it. It was like taking care of a patient. There was no love. The love he felt when he had first met her seemed to have evaporated.

After years, he seemed to feel the same emotion for Leena and wanted to spend more time with her, maybe even have a family with her.

It started to get dark and the rain turned heavy.

"Let's go in and start our work," said Vivek.

Leena looked at him and laughed. "Yes, Sherlock. I totally forgot we came here to investigate. Come on, let's get started."

They walked in and started looking around the living room. From there they moved to the bedrooms, the study, the store, and other places. Vivek ripped apart the place trying to look for a vital clue. He was almost monomaniacally obsessed with catching the Housewife. After three hours of searching, they found nothing.

"I can't go on like this. We don't even know what we are looking for. I am done," said Leena, opening a bottle of wine.

"One thing is sure," Vivek said, "that Amrit did come here every month. The caretaker said he brought different girls with him every time."

"Please don't start that again. I hate to hear or talk about this," said Leena.

Leena wrapped a blanket around her and sat down on the sofa. She offered a glass of wine to Vivek. "You better give those grey cells some rest, Sherlock."

Vivek smiled and sat close to her and sipped the expensive red wine. "This really is a beautiful place. You know most men like me dream about owning such a place."

"You can consider this your home and can come here whenever you want," said Leena. "Does that feel good?"

"No, I hate taking favours and this would be a big one," said Vivek.

Leena looked at him and said, "You kissed me. That meant something to me." She realised what she had said and corrected herself, "I mean, I'm just talking as a friend."

Vivek was quiet. He felt awkward thinking about the kiss. He didn't know what to say. "I'm sorry. It was so sudden. I didn't know what happened to me."

They were quiet for some time. The night had turned cold. Leena wrapped the blanket over Vivek's shoulder. They were slightly tipsy and Leena kept her head on his shoulder, talking about her life and work.

In front of them, on a chair, sat Antara in her spirit form, looking at them. Vivek had told her that he would be going to Satara and Kolhapur for some official work. Here he was, sitting wrapped in a blanket with Leena, with her head resting on his shoulder. It had been easy to track him down.

Antara, in her spirit form, had gone to check on Leena and had heard Manpreet talking about Leena's plan of going to Mahabaleshwar with a reporter.

Vivek had lied to her and lying was cheating. The Housewife considered it a cardinal sin.

The same morning Vivek had been so considerate and loving. He had taken her to the hospital, stayed there, delaying his trip, and then brought her home. Suddenly, it all seemed fake to Antara. He was doing it out of duty or a sense of guilt, definitely not love.

She sat there looking at them talking, laughing, and sharing experiences about their lives. They looked at each other and got lost in a deep, long, and passionate kiss.

Antara was so mad that she wanted to pick up the vase, glass or a table and throw it at them. However, in her spirit form, she couldn't touch anything.

She felt cheated. Vivek had not kissed her like this in a long time. She couldn't take possession of inanimate objects, so the only choice was to take over Leena. She entered Leena's body. She too wanted to feel the deep, passionate kiss. She looked at Vivek and asked him to kiss her again. They were lost in the kiss that lasted longer than the first one.

Leena looked at him with bright, shiny eyes. Antara didn't understand whether he was kissing her or Leena. Vivek seemed lost in his passion and started to caress Leena's body and kiss her neck.

Antara couldn't decide whether to step back or let him continue to kiss. She stayed. Vivek started to remove her clothes and they made passionate love. Vivek was never like this with her. It was usually over in a few minutes. Here, he was licking every bit of Leena and doing things he had never done to her before. She let herself flow with it. It was one of the most erotic moments of her life.

By the end, Antara left Vivek and Leena lying inside the blanket. Antara was smiling and dancing around the house. She was happy and joyous. Then she saw Vivek and Leena with their arms around each other. She stood there staring at them and thought, "Was he making love to me or to Leena?"

Antara realised her husband was in love with this other woman and did not love her anymore.

"He lied to me to come here with Leena and kissed her and made love to her. He has another woman in his life. I am no longer important. I was only meant to stay at home, lost in household chores. The young and beautiful woman has taken my place."

43

The front page of most newspapers carried the picture of Leena and Vivek sitting together cosily inside a blanket. The article talked about a secret love affair between Leena and the senior reporter, Vivek, who had earlier interviewed her. The picture was taken and uploaded to social networking sites by a local photographer in Mahabaleshwar and soon picked up by most media houses.

Antara saw it in the newspaper and was furious. She knew they had been kissing and making love. In fact, she had taken over Leena's body while they had made love. But now it was out in public. She knew the women in her society had enough ammunition with the picture to taunt her for days. "You were the one who gave us advice on relationships and marriage. What happened to your marriage? Look at your husband, he is making out with another woman."

She called up Vivek who was on his way back to Mumbai with Leena. They had seen the picture sent to them by Manpreet on WhatsApp.

"All these are lies. You know how the media works," Vivek told Antara, talking to her on the cell phone. "Even I create such sensational stories to grab headlines. She was unwell so I was trying to help her. In that moment someone clicked a picture. Don't worry, I'll be coming to the house and will meet you. Don't get caught up in that typical housewife mentality."

Leena was on a call with Manpreet.

Manpreet shouted at Leena for getting carried away with "that" reporter, "He's trying to use you, Leena. I told you. Now this is all over the papers. I have been getting calls from the board of directors, media houses and our PR and legal advisors. This can go against you. We might lose out. Even the minister has questions. He says that he can't be sure of your character."

"Are you really sure about the minister's character?" said Leena. "Let them say what they want. I know I'm not wrong. Now don't bug me."

At her house, Antara wept and then started to laugh at herself. "I was the housewife who fought for other housewives targeting rapists, wife-beaters, and cheaters. Now my husband has done the same. What should the Housewife do?"

She closed her eyes and instantly was sitting close to Vivek and Leena in their car. She saw them holding each other, kissing.

Leena looked at him and said, "I hope your wife is not too pissed off?"

"*Arey*, she gets hyper about everything. I'm tired of her."

Antara had tears in her eyes. She sat there looking at them necking and kissing.

"Well, last you told me you guys don't have a child," said Leena.

Vivek nodded sadly. "My wife Antara had some issues and couldn't conceive."

"Last I checked the doctor told me I can still become a mother," said Leena with a smile.

Vivek smiled and kissed her.

"What about your sex life?" asked Leena.

"Non-existent," said Vivek.

"Don't worry, now that I exist in your life," said Leena. "How would you describe our sex life?"

"It's rocking," said Vivek.

"You are my life," said Leena, kissing him on the lips.

Antara was aghast. She felt humiliated and shamed.

44

The moment she stepped out of the car, Leena was surrounded by a large group of television reporters, cameramen and photographers. Questions flew in the air. "Are you in a relationship with Vivek?" "How did this hatred for each other turn into love?" "What is the secret of this hush-hush relationship?" "Are you both planning to get married?" "What were you both doing in Mahabaleshwar?" "Is it true that you have a love child with Vivek?"

Leena turned to look at the journalists and gave them her much-practiced smile. "There are thousands of problems in this country and you are running after me? You should be chasing those politicians and scandals and frauds. Vivek is just a good friend. I was not feeling well and he came to help me. Is there anything wrong with that?"

The media didn't want this boring answer. They were baying for blood and wanted it to be spicy. They scrambled after her as she walked inside the building. The security had to make a chain to stop the hungry hounds. Soon, she was safe inside her office.

Manpreet came running to her. "What is all this, Leena?"

Leena sat on her chair. "Mannu, I might be in love. He's a good guy."

"You know he's a reporter. They only suck for a spicy story," said Manpreet.

"We have decided to get married and have a family," said Leena.

"He's already married."

"Well, he told me it's a non-existent marriage and he has decided to divorce his wife."

At the same moment, Vivek walked inside his house to see a teary Antara. "What have you done? All these women are taunting me that you have found another woman. I got to know it through a newspaper. You know how shameful it is? This is the biggest hurt you have given me."

"Antara, please don't behave like a typical housewife. I told you Leena is only a friend. She was not feeling well so I went there to help her," said Vivek.

"You lied to me. You told me you were going to Satara and Kolhapur while you were there with her in Mahabaleshwar."

Vivek tried to laugh it off. "Yes, I was in Satara, but when I got her call, I went to see her in Mahabaleshwar. It's close by. Is there anything wrong with that?"

"Did you kiss her? Have you made love to her?"

"What are you talking about?"

"I have every right to know it. Tell me, are you in love with her?"

"Antara, please, you are also behaving like those aunties," said Vivek.

"Yes, now I have become like an aunty. After all, you have found a young, sexy, perfect figure girl who is also rich."

"God, enough of all this," said Vivek.

"Haan, why would you listen to me? You

have found a sexy woman to have sex with."

"Are you going crazy or what?"

"I'm not crazy. It's you who is crazy after that businesswoman. Suddenly, this housewife looks boring and ugly and old. What is so special about that woman?"

Antara was almost hysterical, tears gushing out of her eyes.

Vivek stepped closer to her and touched her on the shoulder to comfort her.

"Don't touch me with those hands. Keep those hands for that bitch."

"Hold your tongue," shouted Vivek.

"Why? Why are you so defensive?" shouted Antara and pounced on him, slapping and hitting him on the face, "You told me you don't love her. But you can kiss her and make love to her? You are worse than those men who beat their wives. You are a sly bastard who cheats and lies and sleeps with other women and still tries to carry on with his wife. You are a sick bastard."

At this Vivek gave her a tight slap across her face. "Don't you dare call me names," shouted Vivek with rage.

Antara was stunned. Vivek had never slapped her in all the eleven years of their marriage. Today, he had not only slapped her but abused her and cheated on her because of another woman.

"I gave you all these comforts, this house, car, fixed deposits and security. What did you give me? I wanted a family and you couldn't even give me a child."

Antara stood rooted to the spot, as if all the blood had drained out of her. She couldn't say anything. Vivek kept up with his rant, "You want to know about my relationship with Leena. I'm in love with her and I want to marry her and have a family. So it's better we part ways amicably and get a divorce by mutual consent or I'll have to file a case against you."

With that, Vivek picked up his bag and walked out.

45

Antara looked devastated with her dishevelled hair, tear-stricken cheeks, with a red mark appearing on the side where Vivek's slap had landed. She stood in front of a mirror, staring at her image. She started to remove her clothes one by one and checked herself in the mirror. She grabbed the heavy layer of fat on her stomach and sides. She looked at her thick arms. She turned to look at her heavy butt and thighs. She turned to look at the mirror and held her sagging breasts in her hands.

"What did I give you?" she said with teary eyes. "I gave you my whole life. I gave away my career so you could fly and shine. I turned from a professional into a housewife.

I gave up all my desires and dreams to be with you. I gave up my likes and dislikes to please you. I gave up my family to be with yours. I accepted everything of yours and was never accepted by you and your family. I gave you respect, love, care, trust, my body, my thoughts, my dreams, and my loyalty like a dog. You broke them all, shattered me and my life completely. Just because I couldn't give you a child you discarded me like an old rag."

She kept a hand on her head and gently patted it.

Looking in the mirror she said, "You know, Antara, when we got married, we used to stay in a *barsati* in Delhi. We had these lofty dreams and plans to travel around the world, have a house of our own and have a super happy life. We were young and life was full of possibilities. When we moved to Mumbai and the doctors told me that I couldn't conceive, my whole life collapsed. I started with my IVF treatments and Vivek got busy with his work and assignments and travel. I never travelled anywhere. All my dreams died with that medical report."

Antara tried to hold back her tears, but they kept flowing as her entire married life flashed in front of her like images on a cinema screen.

"If I get angry seeing him with another woman or if I even question him, I am a typical housewife? I wanted to help him in his career and used Leena to give him an exclusive interview. I helped him become a star reporter. Now he has hooked up with that same Leena. Isn't life a bitch, Antara?" She laughed at herself.

She looked at herself and said, "I turned into a crusader against evil men who commit crimes against women, be it rapists, wife-beaters or cheaters. What should I do with my own husband? I loved him with all my heart and he asks me to agree to a mutual divorce. Wow! Fuck off, Mr Vivek Sachdeva. I'll not divorce you."

46

Leena finished her twentieth lap in the pool. She was exhausted after her one-hour workout in the gym and forty minutes of swimming. She was wearing a two-piece and stepped out to pick up the towel when Vivek grabbed her and jumped into the pool. For a moment Leena was taken aback, but then they looked at each other and laughed playfully.

"You scared me," said Leena, hitting him playfully.

"Let me scare you more," said Vivek and pulled her close and kissed her hard on the lips.

"Is that the best you got?" said Leena, teasing him and moved away.

Vivek rushed to grab her and she swam away. Vivek followed.

At the poolside Antara sat on a chair, watching the play. She could see that Vivek was happy with Leena. He was never so playful with her. Instead he always looked sulky, grumpy, and bored with her. Or was he really bored of her?

Vivek swam and caught Leena in one corner and they kissed for long.

Antara kept looking at them. I could leave them to have a happy life and walk away. But what about my life, my sacrifices, my tears and all the love that I had showered on my husband?

Leena and Vivek started to splash water on each other. Vivek jumped at her, pulled off her bikini bra, and swam away with it. Leena chased him and he threw it out. Leena went underwater and came out at the other end, teasing him. Vivek swam towards her. Leena again went underwater but Vivek caught her. They collided, kissed and grabbed each other.

Vivek came out of the water with her panties and showed them like a trophy and threw them out as well. Leena swam towards the opposite side, followed by Vivek. As

Leena reached the other end, she turned and looked at Vivek with bright, shiny eyes and said, "Come to me, Vivek."

As Vivek reached her, she jumped on him and pulled him underwater.

For a moment Vivek thought it was a game, but then Leena pushed him deeper. She put her arm around his throat and started to choke him. They kept going down further and further. Vivek started to lose his breath and soon he was flailing to free himself from her grip. They went down and touched the bottom. Vivek struggled for breath as Leena pinned him down. She looked at him with those bright and shiny eyes. Finally, she smiled and loosened her grip.

Vivek rushed to the top and emerged from the water taking in deep breaths.

Leena came out and smiled at him.

Vivek shouted, "You could have killed me. What's wrong with you?"

Leena came up to him and kissed him saying, "Why are you so angry? What did I do? Come on, be a sport."

Puzzled, Vivek jumped on her saying, "Let me show you how playful you were."

Leena shrieked and tried to swim away, as Vivek grabbed her from behind and both of them started laughing.

Antara stood close by, watching them.

I can't even kill you? For all that talk about avenging cheaters, rapists, and beaters, I fall short in cleaning up my own house. I stop short when it comes to my own cheating husband. I can only hope the near drowning taught you a lesson. You were right. I am just another failed housewife...

47

Antara's mother, Rajshri, was eating golgappas at a roadside stall in Karol Bagh with the retired Colonel eyeing her with a smile when Antara called. She stepped to a side, "Antara, I wish you were here. I am having the best golgappas and that Colonel is close by, smiling at me."

Antara, sitting on the bed, spoke softly, "Mummy, I have decided to stop this IVF treatment and all the hormone injections. I can't do this anymore. I have decided to live without a child."

"What has happened to you? It might happen any time," said Rajshri.

Antara shook her head. "No, Mummy. Now

it will not happen. Why is it that a woman is not considered complete till she has a child? No one questions men. I did everything that I was told to keep my husband happy. All these years you have been giving me tips to look hot and sexy for my husband. You told me to take care of what all he likes and dislikes and I did everything. No one ever asked me what I like or dislike? Even you never asked me."

Antara broke down and cried.

"Antara, *beta*, don't cry. I am your mother and I will always want the best for you. I want you to be happy."

Antara, in between her sobs, said, "I gave up all my dreams to have a family, a child, so that Vivek and I could be happy. I now realize we were never happy. It's good that we don't have a child or he too would be unhappy. Happiness is not some faraway goal. It comes from within. We were constantly looking for it outside. From now on, I'll lead my life the way I have always wanted to. I have lost all these years and for what? In trying to give happiness to my husband, what did I get?"

"*Beta*, what happened? Did you both have an argument? It's part of life. You have to learn to maintain balance and keep moving ahead," said the mother.

Antara almost laughed out sarcastically. "What world do you live in? You have no idea what is happening in the life of your only child. I did try to maintain balance for all these years. I thought we had a lot of love. I never thought my dreams would come crashing down on me."

"Antara, come to Delhi for a few days. We'll talk this out, maybe even have some fun?"

"Yes, I will call you later." And she cut the call.

She called Vivek next. The man was busy driving a Land Rover, his favourite SUV, one that he had always dreamed of. On his meagre salary, he would never have been able to afford it. It was a gift from Leena. She was head-over-heels in love with him and showered him with gifts – expensive watches, designer suits, handcrafted shoes, perfumes and this latest SUV.

It was Vivek's pride and joy. All his dreams were coming true. He might soon have his own news channel and then would expand into entertainment and movies like those big international studios. Suddenly, he was flying high with the presence of the right woman in his life.

He checked his expensive watch and inhaled the perfume he was wearing along with the light fragrance of the SUV's interiors. It was intoxicating. He was high on the smells and the rush of dreams in his head when his mobile rang.

An unknown number. Being the newshound that he was, he answered.

On the other side was Antara calling from a local phone booth near Borivali station. She had stuffed her mouth with tissues to disguise her voice and covered the mouthpiece to muffle the sound further. "This is the Housewife."

Vivek laughed out. "So, Housewife, what's up? What are you up to these days?"

"I'm keeping track of you."

"Don't kill me, please," joked Vivek.

"I did try in Leena's pool. It would have been so easy. The star reporter drowned in the swimming pool of his rich lover," said Antara.

Vivek slammed the brakes, then parked his dream car on the side, stunned at her statement. "Did you make Leena drag me down in the pool?"

"Yes, I did. I can kill you even now and make it look like an accident."

"How do you do this? Do you hypnotize people or what? Will you give me an exclusive? I can make you famous," said Vivek.

"The time for that is gone. You cheated on your wife. You found yourself a young and rich plaything. You forgot your wife who gave up everything for you," said Antara. "You deserve to be punished for being the scum you are."

Vivek got angry. "You know nothing of my life. So what if I am married? Our marriage was already dead. We had nothing in common. We were just dragging along, trying our best to look happy, trying to talk and go out and do things together. It was too much effort."

"What about the time in Goa? What about all the moments you shared at home? Did that mean nothing at all?

"There is no love. I tried. She wanted it. I tried to make her happy. There is no love. Is there anything wrong if a married man falls in love again, especially if his own marriage is dead?"

Antara was quiet.

Vivek went on. "With Leena, I feel alive and happy. We love each other and want to have a life and family together."

Hearing his words, Antara cut the call and walked out, tears streaming down her face.

48

Antara sat looking at her wedding album. The colour photographs were arranged starting from the arrival of the groom, through the various ceremonies till the bride leaves her house. She saw her mother smiling with her large group of Karol Bagh friends. Her relatives looked so happy stuffing their mouth with sweets. She couldn't stop her tears.

She remembered the antics they played during the *jai-maal*. As Vivek stepped ahead to put the garland around her, Antara's friends picked her up and lifted her beyond his reach. Vivek had to be picked up by his relatives to reach her neck. She saw him eyeing her throughout the ceremony. It looked so romantic. It was not a lavish wedding, but all their close friends and relatives were there. There was food and drinks. Vivek's friends created lot of *hulla-gulla*, getting drunk, dancing, hitting on girls and, finally, puking.

She saw each and every face. They all seemed genuinely happy for her. Vivek was a good guy with a good job. He was well-educated and came from a good family. What else does a girl's family want? Her mother was ecstatic. Their love marriage turned into an arranged one, with both families coming together.

Antara couldn't bear seeing anymore happy pictures. She didn't know what to do. Where to go. She cried and cried. She saw another album tucked away in the corner of her cupboard. She took it out. It was filled with old black and white photographs.

She flipped through it to see her childhood. There she was almost five, posing with her mother and father. The moment she saw her father, tears started flowing again. In all these years since he passed away, she had almost forgotten him. She saw pictures where she posed with an ice-cream, behind a cut-out of a car with her father, and standing atop the cardboard moon with her parents.

Seeing these, her entire childhood flashed by in front of her. Her father ran a small cloth store in Chawri Bazaar. Her mother used to help him and take care of all the household chores. Antara was five and a happy child, running in the many lanes of Old Delhi. All the shopkeepers knew her and would gladly offer her sweets, ice-cream, and candies.

She remembered clearly the night when their shop was gutted. The lengthy cloth bundles were all burnt and the shop itself was beyond repair. Her father had rented the shop and had to pay for all the damages. He was left with no money. They had to leave the one-room apartment they rented in Chawri Bazaar.

For a few days, they had stayed with one of her father's friends, but her father decided to move out and start work. They couldn't find any accommodation and finally settled inside a Muslim graveyard in Old Delhi. The caretaker of the graveyard, Yusuf, an old man nearing eighty years, allowed them to stay in a broken hut. The graveyard was strewn with long dried grass and shrubs with thorns. It was difficult to walk through. Even the families had stopped visiting their dead.

Antara's father managed to get some

money and bought a few shawls, blankets, bedsheets, and sarees and started going from house-to-house to sell them.

It was in the graveyard that Antara saw the spirit of a beautiful woman who went gliding over the graves late in the night. Antara ran after her calling her out to play with her. The spirit was surprised to find this little girl who could see her. Soon Antara got friendly with many other spirits who roamed the graveyard at night. There were times when her mother would cook for her and she would bring her food for the spirits to share.

The mother was puzzled and scared, thinking there might be ghosts. What if they possessed her daughter? She got a *taaweez* made from a maulvi and tied it around Antara's arm. Nothing seemed to stop the little girl. She played with the spirits as she ran over the graves and the spirits laughed with her.

Soon the entire graveyard transformed into a beautiful garden. The dried grass gave way to green grass and flowers bloomed. It was the magic of love.

Years later, after being married and having lived as a housewife for years and on the verge of being divorced, Antara could see it clearly. It was late one night that the spirit of the beautiful woman came to her as she played on one of the graves.

The spirit touched her saying, "Finally after years of being caught in this world I've got my salvation, *mukti*, and it's because of you little girl. I lived my entire life as a selfish person who cheated and conned people for my gain. You taught me that the only purpose in life is to share and love. You have filled me with your love and this love has led to my salvation."

Antara, as a little girl, didn't understand anything and smiled at her, "You know, tomorrow my mummy has planned to make kheer for me. I'll get it for all of you."

The spirit looked at her lovingly and touched her on the forehead. "Antara, you have a pure soul. At one point in your life, you will have total control over it. This will become your unique power and strength. You will be able to use this power to help people." With that the spirit dissolved and vanished.

Antara sat there looking at the sepia-tinted images. She had forgotten that incident. Soon after, her father found a small shop in Karol Bagh and wanted to start a cloth shop. Antara's mother had put her foot down. "There'll not be another cloth shop. I'll start a boutique. For that we won't need to stock any cloth. We'll have two tailors and a master to design and stitch."

That was the shop her mother still ran.

As Antara finished college, her father passed away in his sleep one night. Ever since, it had been the mother–daughter team that fought all their battles.

Now, Antara felt alone. She wished her father was here. He would have understood. She had turned into a kind of Super Woman who punished men who committed crimes against women. Vivek had fallen in love with another woman. She had tried to kill him. But he was her husband and she couldn't do it.

"Is it really a crime for a married man to fall in love with another woman?" she wondered.

"It could be true that he was not happy. He was not driving me out of the house or doing anything that would distress me, apart from divorcing me. What's the use of fighting if our marriage is over? Why am I clutching at straws?" thought Antara.

"If he wants a divorce, I'll divorce him,"

said Antara aloud. "I don't even want any alimony. I'll free him to live his love life."

Antara wiped her tears and said to herself, "I'm an educated woman. I can take care of myself. I will find a job. I'll not take a single paisa from him. I'm my mummy's daughter. She too fought and worked all alone after dad was gone. She never gave up. I will not. I'll build a new life for myself far away from here. I'll go away and let him enjoy his life."

She stood up and checked herself in the mirror. "Maybe one last time I can say bye to him."

49

Leena was dressed in a beautiful dress to go out for dinner hosted by the ambassador of Spain. She wanted Vivek to accompany her, but he had refused. "You know the place will be filled with senior media executives. I don't want to give them more fodder for gossip."

"I want to announce our marriage to the whole world," said Leena.

Vivek held her waist and pulled her closer. "Hold on, sweetheart. You know I cannot marry you till I get a divorce from my wife."

"I don't like you calling her your wife. Now, I'm your wife," said Leena.

"Yes, my wifey. I love you and will make sure that we get married soon," said Vivek.

Leena was as excited as a schoolgirl with her first crush. "I can always cancel the dinner and we can go out together."

"Don't forget your work. You have a lot riding on your shoulders. Be a good responsible CEO," said Vivek. "Come on, get going and enjoy the dinner. Make sure those Spaniards don't touch you or I'm going to come and bust their balls."

"My hero," cried Leena jubilantly, kissing him.

"I'll be right here waiting to eat you up," said Vivek, looking into her eyes.

"I'll be back," said Leena in the famous Arnold Schwarzenegger style. She winked at him and was gone.

Vivek stood there lost in thought.

Antara in her spirit form sat in a chair, watching him intently. "I wanted to look at you for some more time before I go away forever. I won't disturb your beautiful life. It's good to see that you are happy and in love. Maybe I couldn't give you what Leena can. She is beautiful, sexy, and rich. She loves you a lot. I'm a fat housewife who couldn't even give you a child. I'll pray you both have a great married life and have a beautiful family together. I wish you all the best. I'll give you the divorce whenever you want. I'll go away from this city and wipe out all the memories. This will be my final gift to you as your housewife."

Just then, Manpreet came rushing into the room. She was dressed in a short dress with high heels and bright red lipstick. "Where's Leena? I told her we are getting late," she called out.

"She just left," said Vivek.

"Damn and she left us alone?"

"All alone," said Vivek and grabbed Manpreet. They looked at each other and kissed on the lips. Vivek started to tear away her dress.

"Slowly, my tiger, let me see what you can do to me," said Manpreet.

Vivek started to remove her dress again as they kissed each other filled with a lust that looked animalistic. Manpreet kissed him, biting, and sucking his lips.

Antara was taken aback. "What? I thought he was in love with Leena."

Vivek and Manpreet were aggressive in their lovemaking, riding each other, trying to dominate each other.

Antara turned her face away, saddened.

Vivek laughed. "Your Leena will be making polite conversation with Spanish people and here you are making hot and sweaty love to me. You are a naughty girl, Manpreet. You need to be taught a lesson."

Antara had no idea what was happening. She had decided to divorce Vivek and let him live a happy life with Leena. But here he was making love to Manpreet. Antara couldn't just make herself get inside Vivek's head and read his thoughts. She would have to wait and see what they were up to.

As they lay spent in each other's arms, Manpreet said, "So what have you planned? How are we going to get rid of Leena?"

"While I was in the pool, I got a brilliant idea. She can easily drown in the pool and die. It could be another suicide," said Vivek.

Antara couldn't believe that Vivek would even think of killing Leena and use the same trick that she had revealed to him.

"That's interesting, or maybe she too can jump off a high rise like Amrit," said Manpreet.

"Another option is a car accident," said Vivek.

"I like the swimming pool one best. It could be another accident. She has already had medical tests done for stress-related issues. It's easier and not messy at all."

Vivek laughed. "If you are going to be the new CEO, what about me?"

"My tiger, you will have your news channel and be the CEO of the entire entertainment division. Does that make you happy?"

"I am waiting to throw my resignation letter at my chief editor and start my own news channel," said Vivek. "I discussed opening a news channel with Leena, but she was against it. She didn't realize that with one news channel we could manipulate the whole country and top politicians would be bowing to us."

"I always knew you were great at creating stories. The way you created a whole new story for Leena was amazing," said Manpreet. "You really went into great detail, creating the new flat. That single key was brilliant, the pictures of girls, and the connection to Mahabaleshwar."

"I had to plan each and every single detail meticulously or Leena might have suspected me. In fact the plan came to me the day that

Housewife called me. I had always suspected that someone had killed Amrit, but her phone call confirmed that and showed me how murders can be turned into suicides. And then I started my work. So a big thank you to you, my dear Housewife, for giving me the brilliant idea. I arranged for the flat, bought the driver, the security guards, planted that key and the pictures. From there on, Mahabaleshwar was easy. The only thing I had to struggle with was to get Leena into her emotional mode so I could hook up with her," said Vivek.

Antara couldn't believe that it was her husband who had manipulated Leena into a relationship by creating the whole façade of the investigation. All the while he was planning with Manpreet to kill Leena and take over her business.

"I was wrong about you. You are worse than a dog," mumbled Antara. I wanted to do everything for you and gave away everything for you. You are even cheating on Leena who is in love with you. You are the worst man I have come across. I wish I could have killed you inside the pool, but the loving, self-sacrificing housewife couldn't."

"You were no less, my Mannu," Vivek

went on. "You kept on messing with her medication, trying to make her feel woozy, out of control, and bent in the head. It will be so easy to finish her now. I have even thought of the headline, 'Super Woman Leena ends her sorry life'."

Vivek and Manpreet laughed.

"I had such a boring life with my wife and now it's become so happening. I'm thrilled about our future together. I planned each and every step meticulously. Finally, everything seems to be falling in place. The last step is to get Leena to make me a partner in the whole business and then quickly get rid of her."

He turned to Manpreet and they kissed.

Manpreet pushed him away, "What about me? Are you not thankful to me?"

Vivek laughed, "My dear Mannu, I couldn't have done it without you. The only good thing about chasing Leena for an interview was that I got to meet you and look how far we have come."

"Leena was my childhood friend. She refused to make me a partner when she took over Amrit's business," said Manpreet. "I put in more work than her. I am good at the job and deserve more for standing by her. But she wanted me to be her pet slave. And I want it all. Now I am going to have it all."

Vivek pulled her closer. "We will have it all."

"But I still want to know how this Housewife managed to kill so many people without ever being near them. Maybe I could have hired her to kill Leena. It would have been so easy," Vivek said.

Antara looked at them as they started another bout of lovemaking. She looked away with teary eyes and vanished.

50

Antara started to clean the house. She did the dusting as she had given the maid a holiday. She looked at the photographs, furniture, wall clock and things they had brought together. She was reminded of their argument when the new refrigerator came. Vivek had wanted to put it in the lobby close to the living room while Antara had put her foot down and insisted that it had to be in the kitchen. She looked at their many pictures on the wall, in photo frames, their moments of joy while eating golgappas, their walks around Colaba, the first time Antara got high drinking Old Monk, and their trips to hill stations. All those memories came floating out of her head.

She walked around the house thinking, *"This is my house, one that we had built to have a happy life. This has turned into my cremation ground, my grave. I wanted Vivek to be happy and have a family with Leena. Look at him, he is even cheating on her and planning to kill Leena. Even the worst of animals don't do that. We humans are capable of evil things. And it had to be my husband."*

She stood in front of her pooja place, looking at the idols of gods and goddesses. "I'm sorry for whatever I have done. I did it as I felt it was right. I'm doing whatever I feel is right."

She wiped her tears and started humming. She stuffed some clothes and her wallet into a bag. She picked up the album with her black-and-white childhood pictures and put it in. She walked into the living room and picked up a photo-frame where both she and Vivek were looking at each other, brimming with happiness. She looked at it and set it down. She walked up to the main light in the hall. She took one last look around and switched off the light.

It was late when Vivek stepped out of the groaning lift and rang the bell of his flat. There was no response.

He kept waiting and rang the bell again. "She's up to one of her surprises again," said Vivek.

Filled with irritation, he continuously rang the bell. He waited and then took out his key and opened the door. It was dark inside.

Vivek stepped inside and closed the door. "Antara, I am not here for any of your dance performances. Please come out. I have had enough of all this nonsense. I want to talk to you, finish this relationship."

No response.

Vivek waited for a whole minute and then extended his hand like always to the switch on the bulb in the living room. There was no Antara there.

She was sitting inside a temple with her back to the wall. The aarti had started and a large crowd of women thronged near the Mata idol. The pujari holding the brass thali with a diya and burning camphor recited the aarti and the women joined in, singing with him.

Antara sat quietly, watching them. She closed her eyes. In her mind's eye, she could see herself back in the house. Before walking out, she had unscrewed the bulb in the living room, put it inside her *chunri* and broken it with the *belan*. She had taken out the filament and screwed it on the holder. She had drawn the curtains, deliberately turning the living room dark. From there she had walked into the kitchen and opened the nozzle of the gas cylinder. With a hiss the gas had spread through the house.

She had stood in the living room, looking around, and walked out of the house, dressed in a salwar-kurta and rubber slippers, holding a single bag.

"I'm going to switch on the light and I don't want to see your item dance." Vivek called out again, with his hand extended.

He took a deep breath. *"What is this smell?"* he thought even as he flicked on the light switch.

The filament of the broken bulb turned red. It took less than a few seconds for the gas to ignite and the whole apartment to blow up.

In the midst of the fire, Vivek saw Antara walking into the room. "What have you done? You blew up our house. Are you crazy? We both will die like this."

"You are already dead, Vivek. This is your spirit standing in front of me."

Vivek looked around to see his burnt body lying on the floor.

"What are you talking? I can't die like this. There's so much I had planned."

"I know you and Manpreet planned to kill Leena and take over her businesses. You are a bastard, Vivek. You deserved to die. I had to kill you or it would be unfair to the other men whom I killed."

"What? Whom did you kill, Antara?"

"I'm the Housewife who killed all those evil men. I called you to warn other men but had no idea that you would turn out to be the biggest scumbag. I gave you so many chances to mend your ways. In fact, I thought I would divorce you and let you marry your Leena and have a happy life. But I had no idea that you planned to kill her till I saw you and Manpreet talking about it."

"When did you see us?"

"At Leena's house. I have this special ability to move my soul out of my body at my will and enter it at will. I killed all those men by taking possession of their bodies or another person's body around them. It was not Leena who pulled you down into the swimming pool, it was me who had taken over her body. I wanted to kill you but then the housewife inside me told me to forgive and forget and let you have a life of your choice. Then I saw you and Manpreet making love and talking about killing Leena. So, finally, I was left with no choice but to kill you."

"I can't be dead," cried Vivek. He tried to touch himself and started to break and disintegrate.

"No no, I can't die like this," shouted Vivek.

"It's time for you to go," said Antara, waving at him.

Vivek's spirit dissolved and vanished.

Antara stood there amidst fire and her burning house for only a few minutes. She had another place to be.

In Manpreet, as she sat at a table, writing a note. She wrote to Leena confessing that all this time she had been cheating on her. That she had planned to kill her along with Vivek and take over her business. She revealed all their plans and their affair. She placed the letter in an envelope and handed it to Leena. Then with a word she turned and walked out...Onto the main road in between the traffic. Suddenly, a speeding van rammed into her.

The hospital she was taken to declared her alive but in a coma. There, in the hospital bed, with her eyes half open, she stared ahead at the soul of Antara.

"God willing, you might wake up from your coma. Till then, goodbye."

Antara, sitting with her back to the wall inside the temple, opened her eyes. She folded her hands, picked up her bag, and walked out.

51

Antara walks in her rubber slippers on the street with a clear head and clear conscience.

As she is walking away, she hears a commotion near the main entrance of a housing society. She walks in to hear that three terrorists have entered the society and taken all the kids hostage. The people outside have informed the police but there is no sign of a police van.

Inside the society, the three terrorists, holding AK-56 rifles, their faces covered, stand around a fearful group of twenty kids. One of them shouts that if their demands are not met, they will start killing a child every hour.

And then, suddenly, he turns to look at his men, his eyes gleaming. He hits one man with the butt of his gun and charges at the other.

"What are you doing? What has happened to you?"

The leader points his gun at them. "Put down your guns or I'll shoot."

The kids are shocked. The other two terrorists don't understand what is going on. The leader warns them again to put down the guns. The men lower their weapons to the ground. The leader shouts at them to raise their hands in surrender. They do as told.

With that, the leader, along with his men, starts to walk out, calling, "We want to surrender."

Just then a police van comes in with armed policemen and they look at the terrorists coming out with raised hands. The leader, too, throws down his gun and raises his hands. The police are shocked. They wait, fearing this might be a signal for something else. Finally, the policemen surround them and only when they all fall on their knees, do they run and pin them down. The kids are safe and their parents rush towards them, thanking God.

Antara, who is sitting on a park bench, opens her eyes and smiles. Her spirit saved the lives of the kids. She too thanks God and the spirit of the beautiful woman who gave her this power to help others.

She gets up and walks by, seeing the terrorist leader shouting at his men, "What happened? How did the police catch us? What did you guys do?" The other two look at him, stunned.

Antara takes her mobile phone out from the bag and calls her mother. "Mummy, I'm coming to Delhi."

Little does she know that there are deadly djinns waiting for the former housewife there.

A former journalist, Mahendra Jakhar is currently an independent screen-writer and author. His first novel, *The Butcher of Benares*, was published by Westland Publications. It was rated as the Best Crime Fiction Debut Novel of the Year and was an Amazon Rising Star. His other books include *The Swastika Killer*, (Westland) and *Chakra Warriors* (Tara Press). Currently, he's developing a web series for Madhur Bhandarkar and wrote the script for *Manjhi: The Mountain Man*. Earlier, he wrote scripts for Mahesh Bhatt, Tiggmanshu Dhulia, Ashwini Chaudhary, Abhinav Kashyap and Hansal Mehta. His film script, *Bhiwani*, based on the boxers of Haryana, was selected for the International Film Festival of India for the Competitive Section at *Film Bazaar*. He conducts workshops on screen-writing and to help discover the hidden creativity, imagination and ideas in everyone.